He Had Never Planned On Being A Father.

But now that Mike was actually faced with the prospect of a child, it was different. Surprising as it was to admit, he had caught himself almost hoping there *would* be a baby. A girl maybe, with Denise's blue eyes and blond hair.

Something inside him shifted painfully. Was it the child he wanted...or was it *her* child that had suddenly become so important?

"We'll know for sure tomorrow," she said, "one way or the other."

He nodded.

"But tonight, Mike," she went on, "let's forget about everything but us. I want one more night with you before we know. Before things change forever."

Mike bit back a groan as an invisible hand tightened around his heart and squeezed. Her quiet words tore at him, leaving his insides open and unguarded.

"Kiss me, Mike."

Dear Reader,

This month Silhouette Desire brings you six brand-new, emotional and sensual novels by some of the bestselling—and most beloved—authors in the romance genre. Cait London continues her hugely popular miniseries THE TALLCHIEFS with *The Seduction of Fiona Tallchief*, April's MAN OF THE MONTH. Next, Elizabeth Bevarly concludes her BLAME IT ON BOB series with *The Virgin and the Vagabond*. And when a socialite confesses her virginity to a cowboy, she just might be *Taken by a Texan*, in Lass Small's THE KEEPERS OF TEXAS miniseries.

Plus, we have Maureen Child's *Maternity Bride, The Cowboy and the Calendar Girl*, the last in the OPPOSITES ATTRACT series by Nancy Martin, and Kathryn Taylor's tale of domesticating an office-bound hunk in *Taming the Tycoon*.

I hope you enjoy all six of Silhouette Desire's selections this month—and every month!

Regards,

Melissa Senate

Senior Editor
Silhouette Books

Please address questions and book requests to:
Silhouette Reader Service
U.S.: 3010 Walden Ave., P.O. Box 1325, Buffalo, NY 14269
Canadian: P.O. Box 609, Fort Erie, Ont. L2A 5X3

MAUREEN CHILD
MATERNITY BRIDE

SILHOUETTE *Desire*®
Published by Silhouette Books
America's Publisher of Contemporary Romance

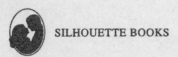 SILHOUETTE BOOKS

ISBN 0-373-76138-4

MATERNITY BRIDE

Copyright © 1998 by Maureen Child

Printed in U.S.A.

Books by Maureen Child

Silhouette Desire

Have Bride, Need Groom #1059
The Surprise Christmas Bride #1112
Maternity Bride #1138

MAUREEN CHILD

was born and raised in Southern California and is the only person she knows who longs for an occasional change of season. She is delighted to be writing for Silhouette and is especially excited to be a part of the Desire line.

An avid reader, she looks forward to those rare, rainy California days when she can curl up and sink into a good book. Or two. When she isn't busy writing, she and her husband of twenty-five years like to travel, leaving their two grown children in charge of the neurotic golden retriever who is the *real* head of the household. She is also an award-winning historical writer under the names Kathleen Kane and Ann Carberry.

One

"**J**ust stick it in, dummy," Denise Torrance whispered to herself and scraped the key across the doorknob plate again. The darkness in the hallway pushed at her. She glanced uneasily over her shoulder and wondered why a simple power outage could make her feel as if she were stuck in a fifties horror movie. For heaven's sake. She knew these offices better than she knew her own apartment. There were no monsters lurking in the shadows waiting to pounce.

"Ah." She sighed in satisfaction as the stubborn key finally slipped into the lock. Pushing her purse strap higher on her shoulder, she shoved the oversize bag out of her way, turned the key and stepped into the darkened office.

Automatically, her right hand went to the switch

plate. She tried each of the two switches with no success. "Perfect," she said into the black stillness. "Apparently, no one is in a hurry to get the power turned back on."

But then, if she had collected the files from Patrick's office a bit earlier, she'd have been gone long before the lights went out and she wouldn't be standing there in the dark talking to herself.

"Ten o'clock at night," she muttered. "What kind of idiot works until ten o'clock when they could be home in a hot bath?"

"Just you and me, I guess." A deep voice rumbled out of the darkness.

Her heart shot into her throat.

"And honey," the voice added, "that bath sounds real good."

She choked her heart back into her chest and whirled around, her gaze sweeping across the shadowy corners of the room. Instinctively, Denise backed up, and wished she was wearing her running shoes instead of the three-inch heels wobbling beneath her. Her sharp eyes strained to find the intruder at the same time her mind screamed at her to run like hell.

Then he stepped closer, passing across a splash of moonlight shining through a window before disappearing into the darkness again. Still, she'd been able to see him. Not his face of course, but enough to know he was big.

And standing between her and the door.

Okay fine, she told herself. No escape there. They were on the third floor, so jumping out the window was quickly dismissed, as well. Think, Denise, think. Frantically, she tried to remember the self-defense lessons she'd taken the year before. Something about step into the attacker and throw him over your shoulder?

Yeah, right.

She took another step back, bumped into a chair and staggered. One of her heels snapped off and she dropped into a tilted stance. "Stay back," she warned, in her best I-am-a-trained-killer voice. "I'm warning you...."

"Take it easy, lady," that voice came again as the man took a step closer.

"I'll scream." An empty threat. Her mouth and throat were so dry, it was a wonder she could issue these whispery warnings, let alone, scream.

"Oh, for..." He sounded disgusted.

She hobbled backward, listing dangerously to one side. Why couldn't she think? Why couldn't she remember *something* that she'd learned from that overpriced instructor? It was just as she'd always feared. When faced with a *real* attacker, her mind had gone blank.

Her purse swung around with her jerky movements and slapped her in the abdomen. She grunted with the impact.

"You okay?"

"Hah!" A concerned maniac! Oh God, she was hyperventilating.

"Look lady, if you'd only stand still for a second..."

"I won't make it easy on you," she countered

and went into a wild series of bobs and weaves. Her broken heel actually helped in the endeavor. She banged her hip on the corner of Patrick's desk and promised herself that if this madman killed her, she would haunt Patrick Ryan for the rest of his life.

Some friend *he* is, she thought hysterically. Taking a vacation so that she would be forced to go into his office and get the files her father wanted for tomorrow afternoon's meeting. If she survived this, maybe she would have her father fire good ol' Patrick.

"Dammit, woman!" The huge man in black sounded angry. Swell.

She started singing to herself. Well, not really singing, more of a low pitched keening, really. Anything to make enough noise that she didn't have to hear the man's voice as he taunted her. Denise took another few steps, then stopped cold as her purse strap snagged on the corner of the desk. Her breath caught, she leaned forward to free herself and at the same time…miraculously, an actual *thought* occurred to her.

Hurriedly, she dug into her purse. She couldn't see well in the dark. She had to depend on her fingers finding just what she needed. Blindly, she began tossing item after item out of her bag and onto the floor.

"Come on now," he urged and came much too close. "If you'll just relax, we can straighten all of this out."

Oh, sure. Relax. *There's* an idea!

Her breath staggering, her heart beating wildly

enough to explode from her chest, Denise's fingers closed around the can she had been fumbling for. Triumphantly, she yanked it free of the leather purse, held it up and pointed it—hopefully—at the intruder. Just in case though, she closed her eyes and turned her head away as she pushed the aerosol button.

"Damn it!" he shouted and lunged at her.

A squeak of protest squeezed past her throat.

He slapped the can out of her grip and his momentum carried her down to the floor with him. They hit hard, but he had twisted them both around until he took most of the jarring blow. Immediately then, he rolled her beneath him. He lay across her, pinning her down with his imposing size and weight.

Helplessly, Denise heard her can of pepper spray hit the plank floor and roll into the far corner. She inhaled sharply, hoping for a good, long scream, then felt a large, very strong hand clamp down hard on her mouth.

The mingled scents of Old Spice, tobacco and what smelled like motor oil surrounded her.

"Take it easy, will ya?" he said angrily.

Yeah, that's what she would do, she thought frantically as she fought to draw a shallow breath into her straining lungs. Take it easy. Simple enough for *him* to say. His body lay full-length atop hers. She felt his belt buckle digging into her stomach and the hard muscular strength of his thighs pressing her legs down.

Why hadn't she gone home when everyone else in the building had?

Her mind raced with questions she didn't really want the answers to. What was he doing in Patrick's office? This was an *accounting* firm for heaven's sake. There was no money to steal. And what was he going to do to her? God, she suddenly remembered every horrifying newspaper article she'd ever read about the rising crime rate.

And now she was going to end up as nothing more than a grainy photograph beside a short sad story on page five.

Even as she thought it, her captor eased slightly to one side of her. Still keeping one of his legs tossed across hers, he captured both of her hands in one of his and held them tightly. As he shifted position, he moved into a patch of moonlight.

Denise closed her eyes and told herself not to look. If she couldn't identify him, maybe he would leave her alone. But somehow, her eyes opened into slits and her gaze drifted to his features anyway.

She gasped and felt a bit of her fear slip away.

He had the nerve to grin at her.

Surprise battled with temper. What was going on here, anyway? Except for his too long hair, a week's worth of stubble on his cheeks and the black leather jacket he was wearing, her intruder looked an awful lot like Patrick Ryan. In fact, she thought with a growing sense of disgust, enough like him to be his...twin.

"Finally," he said and nodded at her. "If you hadn't been so damned eager to spray pepper into my face, I could have introduced myself a while ago."

"You're—"

"Mike Ryan."

"Patrick's twin," she said and tried to twist out of his steely grasp.

"Actually," he countered with a crooked smile, "I prefer to think of Patrick as *my* twin."

Dammit, she thought. Why was Patrick's brother loitering around his office?

"How did you get in here?" she demanded.

"Security let me in."

"Great. Why were you standing around in a pitch dark office?"

He snorted a laugh. "The power went out. Remember?"

"Well, you might have *said* something," she snapped and tried once more to yank free of him. Again, she failed. For some reason, he seemed reluctant to let her go just yet.

"You didn't give me much of a chance."

"There was plenty of time to yell, 'Don't have a heart attack, I'm Patrick's brother'," she countered. Her heartbeat slowed from its trip-hammer pace as she added, "Or do you *enjoy* scaring women?"

He scowled briefly. "There are lots of things I enjoy doing with women," he told her in a voice so deep and rough it scraped along her spine. "Fear has nothing to do with any of them."

She swallowed and found her mouth dry again.

"So," he went on and dragged the palm of one hand over the curve of her hip. "We both know who I am. Who the hell are you? Does Patrick have a girlfriend I don't know about?"

Denise fought to ignore the sensation of wicked heat that trailed in the wake of his hand.

"Maybe," she countered thickly. "But if he does, it isn't me."

"Glad to hear it," he murmured.

She shifted slightly, trying to move away from his disconcerting touch. He followed her.

"Name?" he asked.

"Denise Torrance." She gritted her teeth and redoubled her efforts to get at least one of her hands free. "This is the Torrance Accounting firm. Patrick works for my father. I needed to pick up some of his files... Why am I explaining any of this to you?"

He shrugged. "Beats me. Am I supposed to believe any of it?"

She drew her head back and glared at him. "Frankly, I don't care if you believe me or not. But, why would I lie?"

He shrugged again and let that wandering palm of his slide across her abdomen. Her stomach muscles clenched. Deep inside her, a curl of something dangerous began to unwind.

As if he could read her mind, a deep-throated chuckle rumbled up from his chest.

She felt the flush of embarrassment stain her cheeks and for the first time since entering Patrick's office, was grateful the power was out.

"I don't see a thing funny in any of this," Denise said through her teeth. Especially, she added silently, her body's reaction to him.

"No," he agreed. "I don't suppose you do." As he finished speaking, his hand moved up her rib cage, slipped beneath her sensible linen blazer and strayed dangerously close to her breast.

"Okay, that's it," she muttered, wrenching violently to one side. She wasn't about to lie on the floor being mauled by a virtual stranger…no matter how much her body seemed to enjoy it.

"You son of a—" Denise gave a furious heave and wrenched one hand free of his grasp. Curling her fingers, she drew her arm back and then let it fly. A fist too small to do any damage clipped him across the chin.

Immediately, he released her and Denise rolled far away from him. Scrambling to her feet, she tugged at her wrinkled, pin-striped business suit until she felt back in control. Then she lifted her gaze to his and glared at him.

The bastard had the nerve to *laugh* at her?

Rubbing his chin with one hand, he nodded at her slowly. "Not a bad right, for a girl."

"I'm not a girl. I'm a woman."

"Oh yeah, honey." His gaze swept over her. "I noticed."

The overhead lights flared back into life and Denise blinked, momentarily blinded by the unexpected brightness. When her vision had cleared again, she looked at the man standing so casually just a foot or two away from her.

A relaxed, half smile curved his well-shaped mouth as he watched her. His nose looked as though it had been broken more than once—no doubt by some furious female, she told herself. The whisker stubble on his face gave him a wicked, untamed look, which she was somehow sure he cultivated purposely. His too long black hair hung down on either side of his face and lay across the collar of his jacket. As she looked at him, he reached up with both hands and slowly pushed the mass back out of his way.

Tall and muscular, he wore a spotless white T-shirt beneath the leather jacket that seemed to suit him so well. His worn, faded jeans rode low on his narrow hips and hugged his long legs with an almost indecent grip. Scuffed, square-toed black boots completed the picture of modern day pirate.

She lifted her gaze back to his face and saw sharp green eyes assessing her. It was as if he knew what she was thinking. Amusement flickered in those eyes and she wanted to smack him. Again.

No one should be that sure of himself.

In an instant, his gaze swept over her, mimicking the inspection she'd just given him. Instinctively, she pulled the edges of her navy blazer together and balanced herself carefully on her one good heel.

When his gaze lingered a bit longer than necessary on the fullness of her breasts, Denise shifted uncomfortably. She could almost *feel* his touch on her body. Her traitorous mind wandered down a dangerous path and imagined what it would feel like to have his fingers caressing her bare flesh. At that thought, another onslaught of heat raced through her, leaving her unexpectedly shaky.

"Well," Mike said as he eased down to perch on the edge of his brother's desk. "I've got to say, I've never been hit by anyone as pretty as you."

"I find *that* hard to believe."

He chuckled again and folded his arms across that magnificent chest.

Good Lord, she groaned silently. Magnificent?

"Most woman don't find me as...distasteful, as you do, Denise."

The sound of her name, spoken in that voice, made her knees weak. Instantly, she wished heartily that she was already in the elevator on the way to the parking lot.

"What do you say we try it again?" he asked.

"What?"

"Oh," he nodded congenially at her. "I'll let you hit me again too, if it makes you feel better about enjoying my touch."

"I can't believe you!" Another flush rose up in her cheeks, but this time, she was sure it was just as much anger as embarrassment.

"You can believe me, honey. I never lie to my women."

"I am *not* one of your women."

His gaze raked over her slowly, deliberately, before coming back to stare deeply into her eyes.

"Yet," he said simply.

"You're incredible!" She gasped and fought to ignore the surge of heat flooding her. Something flashed in his eyes and was so quickly gone, she couldn't identify it. But it had almost looked like a teasing glint.

"So I've been told." He pushed away from the desk and took a step toward her. "What do you say, honey?" He rubbed his chin with two fingers and said softly, "That little punch of yours was worth it, you know. To touch you again, I just might be willing to put up with anything."

Her stomach dropped to her feet and her heartbeat hurtled into high gear. She limped backward a step, never taking her eyes from him. She wasn't frightened. At least not of him.

Whether he was teasing her or not, she knew she wasn't in any physical danger from him. He hadn't *had* to let her go. She knew as well as he did that her fist hadn't done the slightest bit of damage to him.

The only thing worrying her now was her reaction to him. Mike and Patrick Ryan were more different than she had at first thought. Oh, they looked alike, there was no denying that.

But she had never experienced this sizzling rush of desire for Patrick. Not once had she imagined rolling around on the floor of his office with him…burying her fingers in his hair…feeling the scrape of his whiskers against her skin.

As those images rocketed around in what was left of her brain, she took another uneven step back in self-defense. What in the world was happening to her? Only moments ago, she had been fighting him, sure that he was some maniac out to destroy her. Now, she trembled at the thought of being kissed senseless by that same maniac?

Oh, she was in big trouble.

Mike smiled. A slow, seductive smile that told her he knew where her thoughts were going.

And that he approved.

Short, shallow breaths shot in and out of her lungs.

She grabbed at the remaining bulk of her shoulder bag and clutched it in front of her as though it were a magic shield, designed to keep lechers at bay. Her fingers worked the leather, locating her wallet and car keys. One corner of her mind realized just how much of her stuff she'd thrown onto the floor. Her purse only weighed about half as much as usual.

The hell with it, she thought, keeping one eye on the man opposite her. She could get the rest of her things later.

"I'm leaving now," she said and took another hobbling step. "I assume, since you're Patrick's brother, you're not here to rob the place?"

"Good assumption," he countered and moved a bit closer.

"Then why are you here, anyway?"

"How about we go get a drink and get acquainted?" Mike asked and took another step toward her. "I'll tell you everything you want to know about me."

All she wanted to know was why he had such a strange affect on her. But she wasn't about to ask him *that*.

He smiled at her again.

Run, her brain screamed. Run now, before it's too late.

It was the rational thing to do.

It was the only thing that made sense.

So why did a part of her want to stay?

"What do you say?" he repeated. "A drink?"

He reached out one hand toward her.

Denise looked from that hand to his eyes and shook her head, more disgusted with herself than she was him. She mentally shoved her raging hormones aside. "Ryan," she said slowly and distinctly, "if this was the Sahara and you had the only map to the last Oasis in existence, I *still* wouldn't have a drink with you."

Then she turned and clomped inelegantly from the room and down the hall with as much dignity as she could muster under the circumstances.

As the elevator doors slid soundlessly closed behind her, she heard him laughing.

Two

Mike stood in the doorway looking after her for a long moment, then turned around to stare at the mess strewn across his brother's office. In her hurry to find her pepper spray, Denise Torrance had thrown the contents of that huge purse of hers all over the room.

He snorted another laugh and shook his head. Next time he volunteered to fix his twin's air conditioner, he'd make sure to find out if there was going to be a pint-size tornado dropping by.

Of course, if the tornado happened to have short blond hair, wide blue eyes and a dusting of freckles across her nose, he wouldn't work too hard to avoid her.

From down the hall, he heard the discreet hum of the elevator as it carried her farther away. He'd thought about chasing after her, but then realized that he didn't have to.

He'd see her again.

As he bent and scooped up some of her belongings to stack them neatly on the desk, he muttered, "She has to come back. Hell, she left half of her life behind."

Quickly, he went around the room, snatching up the items she'd tossed. As he grabbed the can of pepper spray, he winced and told himself it was a damn good thing he was quicker than she was. He almost set the can with everything else, to be returned to her, then thought better of it and stuffed it into his jacket pocket instead. No sense in arming the woman, he told himself.

He placed the last of her things on the desk and took a long look at them. Everything from a hairbrush to a tube of toothpaste and a neatly capped toothbrush sat atop the mahogany surface. Shaking his head, he noted the foil-wrapped sandwich, a package of Ding Dongs, a screwdriver set and a package of bandages. But then his gaze fell on the jumbo-size bottles of aspirin and antacid tablets, two black eyebrows lifted high on his forehead.

Ms. Denise Torrance apparently led a *very* stressful life.

Even as he wondered why, he told himself that it was none of his business. He made it a point never to know too much about anyone. With knowledge, came caring. With caring, came pain.

A small, shiny object on the floor caught his eye and he leaned over to pick it up. His long fingers turned the key over and over as he studied it. A smile crept up his features and he glanced at the wall of file cabinets across the room from him.

The only way she was going to get back into this office was with a key. And she'd left hers with him.

Folding the key into his palm, he pocketed it, then walked back to the faulty air-conditioning unit in the corner.

Whistling softly, he told himself that just because he wasn't going to get involved, that didn't mean he had to avoid her completely. Besides, anyone so stressed out that they carried enough medication to dose a battalion was desperately in need of some relaxation.

As he pried the metal cover off the unit, he smiled. It would be his distinct pleasure to introduce Denise Torrance to a little fun.

In the soft morning light, Denise stood outside the brick-and-glass building and stared at the foot-high letters painted on the front window.

Ryan's Custom Cycles.

That unsettled feeling leapt back into life in the pit of her stomach and she sucked in a gulp of air, hoping to quiet it. It didn't work.

Her fingers clenched and unclenched on the soft, brown leather of her shoulder bag. It hadn't been hard to locate Mike. Patrick had once mentioned his twin's motorcycle shop, so a quick glance through the yellow pages had been all the help she had needed.

Denise's stomach lurched and she laid one palm

against her abdomen in response. "Stop it," she muttered. "He's just a man." And, her mind quietly jabbed, the Statue of Liberty is a cute little knick-knack.

"Oh, for heaven's sake!" She admonished herself as she started across the parking lot. She didn't have all day. Her first meeting of the morning started in less than forty minutes. Her father, as president of the firm, would be there and he wasn't the kind of man to accept excuses for tardiness.

Denise groaned. Just thinking about having to face her irate father this early in the morning was enough to churn up the acid in her stomach. Rummaging in her purse, she yanked out a small roll of colored tablets and popped two of them into her mouth.

As she chewed, she told herself that she didn't have much choice in this. She *had* to see Mike again. "Of course," she said under her breath, "if I hadn't let him bully me into running for cover last night, this wouldn't be happening."

But she *had* allowed it. Not until she was halfway home had she remembered that she'd left behind Patrick's spare key and the files she had needed. She had also forgotten about the things she'd thrown out of her purse in her wild search for pepper spray.

"Pepper spray, self-defense classes," she grumbled in disgust. "A fat lot of good they did me."

Too late to worry about that, though. She stopped in front of the sparkling clean glass door and took a deep, calming breath. Then she pushed the door open and stepped into another world. A world where she obviously didn't belong.

The showroom was immense.

Her gaze flew about the room, trying to take it all in at once. Blond pine paneling covered the long wall behind the room-length counter. On the side wall, glass-fronted shelves displayed everything from helmets to gauntlet-style black gloves to black leather pants and boots. The opposite wall appeared to have been designated an art gallery. Against the soft, cream paint were bright splashes of colored signs, proclaiming the name, Harley-Davidson. Beneath those signs, stood racks of clothing. T-shirts, jackets, chaps, even ladies' nightgowns, all with the same Harley-Davidson logo.

But the most impressive display were the motorcycles themselves. Gleaming wood floors mirrored the chrome surfaces of the almost elegant-looking machines parked atop it. Sunshine filtered through the front and side windows, sparkling off the metal, glinting against the shining paint jobs.

Denise shook her head, dazzled, in spite of herself. Somehow, she had expected a find a dirty, oil-encrusted garage where beer-swilling mechanics scratched their potbellies and traded dirty jokes.

A long, low whistle caught her attention and her head snapped around.

"How did *you* slip in here, honey? Are you lost?"

The big man in worn jeans and a flannel shirt scratched at his full beard and grinned at her.

She tugged at the front of her sea green blazer and tightened her grip on her purse. All right, so maybe she *did* look out of place. She glanced around the room again, noting the sprinkling of customers for the first time.

Only a handful of people were in the store and *none* of them were in a green silk business suit. Except of course, Denise. And, they were all staring at her as though she'd just been beamed down from the planet Stuffy.

Apparently, she thought, as the people went back to what they had been doing when she entered, jeans and black leather were the preferred costume of motorcycle enthusiasts. Even for the women, she told herself as she spotted the only other female in the room.

A pang of envy rattled around inside her as she noted the tall blond woman's long, straight hair and skintight jeans. Without benefit of a shirt, her black leather vest looked provocative. Dismally, Denise acknowledged that even were she to wear the same outfit, the results would be very different. A quick glance down at her own, less than impressive bustline confirmed the thought.

"Looking for a bike, lady?"

She turned toward the first man again. "No." She cleared her throat and told herself to remember why she was there. It didn't matter if she would look terrible in a leather vest, since she had no plans to acquire one. "Actually, I'm looking for Mike Ryan."

He nodded, then said wistfully, "Too bad." Jerking his head toward the door behind the counter, he added, "Mike's in the service bay. He'll be back in a minute."

"Thank you."

A moment later, that door opened and Mike stepped into the room. Denise's stomach jumped. She ignored it and walked toward him.

"Nice wheels," the bearded man said.

She stopped and looked at him. "What?"

"Your legs, Denise," Mike spoke up and shot a telling look at the other man. "He said you have nice legs."

"Oh." Flustered a bit, she nodded and said, "Thank you very much."

Hell, Mike thought, what did he care if Tom Jenkins looked at her legs or not? He ignored the skitter in his gut, slapped both hands down on the countertop and leaned forward as Denise came closer.

Dammit, he'd been hoping that he had imagined most of the instant attraction he had felt for her the night before. His gaze raked over her quickly, thoroughly, as she marched determinedly across his shop.

Just his luck, he thought. Even in a boxy, green suit jacket and too long skirt, she did things to him he would have thought impossible at this time yesterday. From the sound system overhead came the muted strains of the Eagles. But over that familiar music, came the sharp click of her high heels against the floorboards. They seemed to be tapping out a rhythm that screamed silently in his head, "Take her, she's yours. Take her, she's yours."

His body tightened and he gritted his teeth in an

effort to ignore the voices and concentrate on the woman. Even though he'd been expecting to see her again, he hadn't expected to feel such a rush of pleasure.

It's nothing, he told himself. At least nothing more than a very healthy response to a pretty woman. It had been a long time since he'd confused hormones with something deeper.

"Morning," he said as she came to a stop opposite him.

"Good morning."

He watched her nervous fingers playing with the strap of her bag. Good. That gave him the upper hand in whatever was going to be between them. And he knew already that there would definitely be *something*.

"What can I do for you, Denise?" he asked, despite the fact that he knew damned well why she was there.

She inhaled sharply, glanced to either side of her to make sure no one was near, then said, "When I left Patrick's office last night, I forgot to take the spare key with me."

"And the files you needed," he added.

"Yes..."

"Oh, and all that junk from your purse."

She frowned. "That, too."

"I know." He smiled at her and saw temper flare in her eyes before she battled it down again.

"You're not going to make this easy," she said quietly. "Are you?"

"Nope."

Her lips thinned a bit, the only sign of her agitation. "Why not?"

"What would be the fun in that?" he asked.

"Does *everything* have to be fun?"

He gave her a long, slow smile. "If we're lucky."

She sucked in a gulp of air and laid her palms flat on the counter, just an inch or so from his. He thought about touching her, but decided to wait.

"Look, Mike. I just want to retrieve that key, get back into Patrick's office and pick up my things." She looked him dead in the eye, hoping, no doubt, to convince him with her calm appeal to his better nature.

Too bad he didn't have one.

He should do what she wanted, he told himself. Just give her back her stuff and let her disappear from his life. He didn't want any entanglements. He wasn't interested in love or long-term relationships. Mike had learned the hard way that love was an invitation to pain and he wanted no part of it. Besides, Lord knew, he had no business getting any closer to a woman who practically had *conventional* stamped on her forehead.

Still, something inside him just couldn't seem to let go. To let it…whatever *it* was between them… end just yet.

"I'll make you a deal," he said instead.

"What kind of deal?" Her head cocked to one side and she looked at him through the corners of *very* cautious eyes.

"Here's the key for Patrick's office and the files, but to get the rest of your stuff you have to go to dinner with me tonight.'' Even as he said it though, he knew dinner wouldn't be enough. He wanted to be alone with her again. Somewhere quiet and dark, where he could kiss her, touch her. And discover if the sensations that had tormented him long after she had stormed away from him the night before were real...or just a product of the unusual situation they had found themselves in.

''Dinner?''

''Yeah.''

''Where?''

''My choice.''

Her toe tapped against the floor. He watched her as she mentally went over the possibilities. She threw him a worried glance and he knew she was thinking the same thing he was. That here was their chance to prove that absolutely *nothing* had happened between them the night before.

Then she surprised him.

''You know,'' she said thoughtfully, ''Patrick never mentioned this ruthless streak of yours.''

He widened his stance and folded both arms across his chest. ''I'm not ruthless, honey. I just live my life on my terms.''

''Which are?''

She wouldn't understand his terms, he told himself. To understand, she would have had to have been sitting in the desert sun, listening to gunfire. She would have had to watch friends die. She would have had to experience the one inescapable fact that life is short. Too damned short.

Since it was pointless to try to explain all of that, he said only, "The terms vary from day to day."

"Now, why doesn't that surprise me?"

He gave her points. Irritated and frustrated, she still gave as good as she got.

"So," Mike said. "What about dinner?"

"Can't you just give me my stuff?"

"I could...but I won't."

Her lips thinned and that toe of hers started tapping even faster. Finally, after she checked her narrow-banded gold watch, she spoke.

"All right, dinner. Here's my address." She dug into that saddle bag she called a purse and came up with a business card. She set it down and took a step back from the counter. "Of course, it's not like I have a choice, is it?" she asked. "To get my things back, I have to go."

"True," he agreed and ignored the small stab of conscience.

"Do you always use extortion to get a woman to have dinner with you?"

"Only when I have to. Like I said, the terms vary. Seven-thirty."

"Seven-thirty."

"You don't have to go, Denise," he heard himself say. "You *could* call Patrick and whine until he agrees to rescue you from me."

One pale blond brow lifted. "First, I don't whine. Second, I don't need anyone to rescue me from you, Mike Ryan. I can take care of myself."

She really was something else. He rubbed his chin thoughtfully and grinned at her. "I remember."

"Good," she said as she turned for the door. "It'll be better for both of us, if you keep on remembering."

What do you wear to have dinner with a man who dresses like a B movie from the fifties and has far more self-confidence than any three people deserve?

Denise stood in the foyer of her condo and checked her appearance in the full-length mirror one more time. Her navy blue dress looked perfect, she thought and swayed to watch the full skirt swirl around her legs.

Nodding to herself, she said aloud, "You wear something that gives *you* confidence, naturally."

She smoothed her fingertips along the modestly cut neckline. Revealing just a glimpse of her collarbone, the long-sleeved dress looked demure, almost prudish, until one saw the back. Smiling to herself, Denise half turned and looked into the mirror over her shoulder. The deeply scooped back dipped sensuously low, coming to a stop just below her waist. The smooth expanse of flesh it displayed was evenly tanned a warm, golden brown.

Denise fluffed her hair one last time, checked the hooks of her sapphire drop earrings, then reached into her tiny evening bag for her lipstick. Though the small, black leather envelope on a slim gold shoulder chain looked lovely, she did miss having her day purse.

Leaning toward the mirror, she carefully lined her lips in a dark rose color, then dropped the tube back into the bag.

"Well, I'm ready," she told herself. "Where is he?"

A quick glance at the clock behind her and she smiled ruefully. Only 7:20. Whatever was wrong with her? She hadn't *wanted* to go on this... She refused to call it a date, even to herself. "So why am I ready and waiting ten minutes early?"

She caught her own eye in the mirror and looked away again quickly. Denise wasn't sure she wanted to know the answer to that question.

A rumble of thunder sounded outside and she winced. Looking heavenward, she muttered, "Give me a break, okay? No rain tonight?"

But the thunder continued grumbling until it rolled up in front of her house and stopped.

Frowning, she opened the door.

"Good God."

Three

Denise stepped onto the porch, pulling the front door closed behind her. She twisted the knob, making sure the lock had set, then started down the pansy-lined walk to the street.

In the hazy, yellowish glow of a streetlight, Mike sat, straddling the biggest motorcycle she had ever seen. Painted bloodred and black, it would have looked intimidating had it been parked and silent. As it was, its engine rumbled like a growl coming from the chest of some jungle beast waiting to pounce.

The word *intimidating* didn't even come close to describing it.

Mike pulled his shining black helmet off and set it on the seat in front of him and Denise took a moment to study him. Dressed entirely in black, he looked even more like a pirate than he had the night before. And was, if possible, even more dangerously attractive.

His hair was pulled back into a ponytail at the base of his neck and, she noted nervously, he had shaved for the occasion. When he turned to look at her, his pale green eyes widened in appreciation, then narrowed thoughtfully.

"It looks great," he admitted. "But it's not what you usually wear on a bike."

"I didn't expect to be riding a bike," she said, although why she hadn't considered it, she didn't know. "We could take my car," she suggested.

"No, thanks. I don't do cars." He reached behind him to the tall bar rising up at the end of the narrow seat. Quickly, he undid the elastic ropes, freeing a silver-and-black helmet, then turned around to hand it to her. "Here. You have to wear this."

"Mike, I…" Sighing, she pushed the helmet back at him. So much for her spectacular dress. "I'll go change."

"No time," he said. "We're going to be late as it is."

"I can't ride that…" she waved one hand at the motorcycle, then at her dress "…in *this*."

His lips twitched in what might have been a smile if given half a chance. But it was gone in the blink of an eye.

"It'll be all right," he said. "Just stuff the skirt between your legs and mine. Keep it out of the spokes."

This was a first. She had never had a man tell her to stuff her skirt between her legs before. Lovely.

"Can't you just give me three minutes to change?" she asked.

He snorted a muffled laugh. "There isn't a female alive who can change clothes in three minutes, honey. And like I said, we're already late."

His expression told her there was no sense debating the issue a minute longer.

"For heaven's sake," she muttered and threw one last, longing glance at her condo, behind her.

"Come on, honey," he told her and pulled his own helmet on. "Just swing one of those gorgeous legs over the saddle and plop down."

Gorgeous?

He released the kickstand and stood up, balancing the bike between his thighs. His hands twisted the grips on the handlebars and the powerful engine grumbled in response.

She couldn't help wondering what her neighbors were thinking at that moment. She could almost feel their interested gazes peering at her from behind the draperies. Well, what did she expect, going to dinner with a man who looked like he'd be back later that night to burgle houses?

He revved the engine again to get her attention.

Then something else occurred to her.

"Hey," Denise shouted over the rumbling engine, "wait a minute."

He looked up at her. "What?"

"Where's my stuff?" She wasn't about to go

through with this little deal of theirs if he hadn't brought her things with him.

Mike scowled, reached back and patted a dark red compartment hanging off the left rear fender. "It's all there," he assured her. "Now, get on."

Gamely, Denise balanced on her right foot and swung her left leg across the motorcycle. Scooting around until she was comfortable, she braced the toes of her Ferragamo pumps on the foot pedals provided and bunched her skirt into the V between her legs. Muttering under her breath, she pulled the helmet on, winced at just how heavy it felt, then secured the chin strap. She didn't even want to think about what her hair was going to look like later.

Then Mike sat down in front of her, easing her thighs farther apart with his black-denim-covered behind. She stuffed her skirt between them, hoping the pooled fabric would dull the heat arcing between their bodies.

The engine beneath her shuddered and throbbed, and something deep in her core began to shake in response.

"Hang on to my waist," he said over his shoulder.

She nodded before realizing he wasn't looking at her. Rather than try to talk over the noise of the engine though, Denise wound her arms around his waist, pressing herself close to his back.

He tossed a glance at her, then reached around and snapped her visor down. "You ready?" he shouted.

She nodded again, but as they pulled away from the curb, she told herself she wasn't ready.

Not for him.

When he shut down the engine, the silence was soul shattering.

Denise climbed off the motorcycle and staggered unsteadily for a moment. Her legs felt as if they were still shuddering in time with the engine of the beast that had brought her here. Undoing the strap, she pulled her helmet off and handed it to Mike. Her head felt twenty pounds lighter as she fluffed her hair, hoping to revive it.

She shivered as a sharp, cold ocean wind swept across Pacific Coast Highway and swirled around her like icy fingers tugging at her. The hum of traffic on the busy highway faded away as she studied the restaurant Mike had chosen.

She'd seen it before, of course. No one living in Sunrise Beach could have overlooked it. Denise had even heard that the city fathers were talking about making it an official landmark.

It looked as though it had been standing in the same spot for a hundred years. The wooden walls looked shaky, the hot pink neon sign across the door, a couple of spots either dimmed with age or broken, spelled out, O'D ul s. Five or six pickup trucks were parked in the gravel lot, but there were more than twenty motorcycles huddled in a tight group near the front of the building.

As she watched, Mike pushed his own bike into their midst.

She had managed to avoid entering O'Doul's Tavern and Restaurant all of her life. Even though she had been tempted to go inside once or twice since turning twenty-one eight years ago, the thought of her father finding out she'd been there had been enough to dissuade her of the notion.

"Ridiculous," she muttered, "a grown woman afraid to stand up to her father."

Unfortunate, but true. All Richard Torrance had to do was look at her with disappointment and she felt eleven years old again. An eleven-year-old girl whose mother had just died, leaving Denise alone with a father who expected perfection from a child too frightened to deliver anything less.

Denise supposed there was some kind of logic in the fact that it would be Mike Ryan to first take her to O'Doul's. Because Richard Torrance would never approve of him, either.

While she waited for Mike, she studied the old tavern-restaurant claim to fame. Their mascot. Good luck charm.

On the rooftop was a fifteen-foot tall, one-eyed seagull, holding an artificial dead fish in its beak.

"Oh yeah, your dress will fit right in, here," she muttered under her breath.

"You know," Mike said as he walked up beside her, "I've noticed you do that a lot."

"Do what?"

"Talk to yourself."

An old habit, born of loneliness. But he didn't need to know that. "It's when you argue with yourself that you're in trouble, Ryan."

"If you say so."

She nodded at the huge bird. "Now I understand why you were in such a hurry to get here," she said. "Reservations must be hard to come by."

"Obviously, you've never eaten here before."

"No, I generally make it a practice only to eat at restaurants where the giant bird has both eyes intact."

His lips quirked. "Vandals. Some kids with rocks and no values mutilate poor old Herman and you blame the bird?"

"Herman?" She smiled, in spite of her best efforts.

With a perfectly straight face, he said, "Herman Stanley Seagull. Jonathon Livingston's big brother."

"Very big."

He grinned.

A moment later, she nodded. "I get it. Stanley...Livingston."

"And I thought you had no sense of humor."

"I'm here, aren't I?"

His eyebrows arched. "A bit touchy, are we?"

"Not touchy," she countered. "Just...cautious."

He laughed shortly. "An accountant? Cautious? There's a shock."

She had heard any accountant joke he could possibly come up with. Personally, she thought that the members of her profession were as unfairly maligned as lawyers. More so, since lawyers usually *deserved* the ribbing they took.

"Well," she said, with another look at Herman, "I hope the food's better than the ambience."

He chuckled. "Don't be a snob, honey. O'Doul's serves the best pizza in town. And if you don't get here early, it's all gone."

"Gone?" Denise stared up at him. "What kind of way is *that* to run a business? Won't he make more food if his customers demand it?"

Mike shrugged. "He could, but then he wouldn't have time to play pool with his friends."

"Of course," she said, nodding slowly. "A man has to have his priorities, after all."

This time, he laughed outright.

But when she started walking toward the restaurant, Mike's laughter died. He had thought it was torturous, with Denise sitting behind him on the bike. Every turn he had made, her thighs pressed harder against his. He'd felt the swell of her breasts pushing into his back and the surprisingly strong grip of her slender arms around his waist. Never had the ten-mile drive to O'Doul's seemed so long.

But all of that was nothing compared to what he felt now. As if a fist had slammed into his belly, his breath left him in a powerful rush the moment his gaze locked on the smooth, tanned surface of her back.

His gaze followed the column of her spine and rested on the curve of her bottom. His palms itched to stroke that expanse of flesh and then to explore further, beyond the boundaries of that incredible dress.

Mike's groin tightened uncomfortably, and he had

to muffle a groan as he gripped the chin straps of their helmets in one hand. He took three long strides and caught up to her easily. Taking Denise's arm with his free hand, he said, "You should have warned me about that dress."

She stopped and looked up at him. A knowing smile curved her lips, but she asked anyway, "What do you mean?"

What could he say? He wasn't about to admit to her what that dress did to him. Nor, he thought with a glance at O'Doul's front door, did he want to think about the impact that dress would have on the men inside. His gaze shifted to her again and Mike found himself staring into those deep blue eyes. After a long moment, she looked away and he took the opportunity to bring himself back under control.

"Let's just say, I like a good tan. Especially when there aren't any suit lines."

She only smiled and Mike's racing brain took care of the rest. Immediately, he imagined her nude, lying under the hot sun. And in his mind, he was right beside her, smoothing lotion onto her warmed skin. He could almost feel her soft, pliant flesh beneath his fingertips.

Great. Now he had *that* mental image to drive him nuts all night.

Steering her toward the door, he grumbled through gritted teeth, "C'mon. I'm hungry."

The fact that he was hungrier for tanned, smooth skin than he was for pizza, had nothing to do with anything.

She should have gone to O'Doul's years ago.

If she had guessed just how much fun the game of pool could be, she might have risked her father's ire. Of course, she wasn't sure if it was the game, or her teacher that she was enjoying so much.

She bent at the waist, set her left hand on the worn, green felt and laid the tip of her cue stick between her curled fingers. Behind her, Mike stood close and leaned over her, his right hand on hers, his chest pressed to her naked back.

Warmth seeped through him down to her bones and she felt the unmistakable, hard bulge of his groin against her behind. She swallowed and tried desperately to listen to what he was saying.

"Take your time, honey," Mike whispered near her ear. "We've got all night to line this shot up."

All night. She inhaled the scent of Old Spice and wondered why more men didn't wear the old-fashioned cologne. Spicy and cool and sexy, it seemed to be everywhere, drawing her deeper into fantasies she had no business indulging and even less of a chance of experiencing.

He worked the pool cut back and forth between her fingers and instead of pool, her mind was caught on another mental image created with that smooth, in-and-out motion.

Glancing to one side, she noticed a biker Mike had called Bear, watching her with knowing eyes. Like the other men in the place, he wore jeans and leather and a leering expression that would have worried her if not for Mike's presence. She turned her gaze back to the pool table in time to see her stick make contact with the cue ball.

Laughter rose up around the table as the white ball missed its mark by inches. Mike straightened up and Denise, suddenly so warm she could hardly breathe, took a step away from him.

"Hey Mike," one of the men called over the pounding, pulsing beat of the music, "losin' your touch?"

"Doesn't look like it to me," a woman in the crowd answered for him. More laughter and Denise was grateful for the smokiness of the room. Hopefully, it was enough to hide the flush she felt staining her cheeks.

The other man in the game, someone called Stoner, took his shot and missed.

"Our turn," Mike said over the music and waved her back to the table.

"I think I'll just watch for a while," she said with a shake of her head. "You finish the game."

"Sure?"

She nodded, knowing damn well the only reason she was quitting was because she didn't know if she could take being that close to him again.

Denise held her pool cue and watched Mike pick up another stick and work his way around the green felt table. He paused every other step or so to exchange some comment with one of his friends and each time he smiled, the knot in her stomach tightened.

She swayed a bit unsteadily and tightened her grip on the stick in her hands, using it more for balance than anything else. Apparently, the beer she'd had with her pizza—the best pizza she'd ever tasted—had gone right to her head. Fog nestled in her brain and Denise struggled to clear it. Of course, the loud rock music blasting over the speakers, the crowded press of bodies in the place and the heavy cloud of blue-gray cigarette smoke wasn't helping things any.

A huge man with tattooed forearms the size of ham shanks slapped Mike on the back in a friendly gesture that would have sent any other man sprawling to the sawdust-covered floor.

Not Mike.

The black T-shirt he wore hugged his shoulders and upper arms, defining muscles that seemed to have a life of their own. They rippled and shifted whenever he took a shot and Denise caught herself holding her breath to watch the show in admiration.

Foggy brain or not, she knew enough to realize that she was in deep trouble.

A moment later, the pool game ended when Mike sank the eight ball in a corner pocket. Cheers erupted and a dark-haired woman in jeans tight enough to cut off her circulation wrapped herself around Mike like a child's grubby fist around a Popsicle stick.

Except that there was nothing childlike about the voluptuous brunette.

When the woman grabbed Mike's face between her palms and planted her lips on his in a long, lusty kiss, Denise gritted her teeth and fought down the roiling in her stomach. She told herself that she had no claim on him. That it didn't matter *who* he kissed.

Or when. Logically, she knew that this wasn't even a real date.

But logic had nothing to do with what she was feeling.

Mike pulled his head back, patted Celeste's shoulder and peeled her off him. He shot a quick look at Denise's tight features and felt...guilty, for God's sake. Stupid. He didn't owe her anything. He wasn't her boyfriend—or God forbid, her husband. And the knowledge that he had no intention of getting involved didn't do anything to quiet the storm inside him.

While he gave Celeste a gentle push toward her date for the night and walked toward his own, he told himself that Denise had no claim on him. He was as free as old Herman, up on the roof.

The fact that Herman was not real and permanently attached to the wooden building was beside the point.

When he reached Denise's side, he took the pool cue from her and passed it off to another player.

"I don't want to interrupt your *fun*," she said loudly, to be heard over the music.

Sure you do, he thought. The look in her eye would have sliced Celeste to ribbons if the other woman had been aware of it. But he didn't say that. Instead, as he heard the music change, he grabbed her hand and headed for the postcard-size dance floor.

She dragged behind him as he wended his way through the Friday night crowd. Once, she even tried to slip away, but he tightened his hold on her and kept walking. When he reached the small area where two other couples were already swaying in time to the music, he stopped and turned around to face her.

Her expression was mutinous, but he didn't give a damn. He'd put up with the other men in the place ogling her all night and now, he wanted the chance to put his arms around her and hold her close. He wanted to show the rest of them that Denise was his.

At least for tonight.

He tugged her closer and she moved slowly, reluctantly.

"Dance with me," he said into her ear and inhaled the delicate, flowery scent of her perfume.

She pulled her head back and looked up at him.

Their gazes met and locked together. A heartbeat of time passed and in that instant, something flashed in her eyes. Mike couldn't identify it and at the moment, didn't want to. All he wanted was this one dance.

For now.

The old song smoothed over the crowd and here and there, a voice picked up the words and sang along. The melody was sad, the lyrics lonely and most of the regulars at O'Doul's could identify with it all too easily. Every desperado in the room felt as though the song were meant especially for him.

Then Denise stepped into his arms and followed as he led her around the floor. Mike bent his head close to hers, relishing the softness of her hair on his cheek. The summery scent of her. The smooth, warm flesh of her back beneath his hand.

The music surrounded them, caressing them as

they moved in tandem, as if they had danced to-gether hundreds of times.

She laid her head on his chest. His palm slid across her back, caressing, with strokes as gentle as the song they danced to. She sighed against him and he cradled her closer.

As the Eagles song swelled to its finish, Denise tipped her head back to look at him. He stared into the depths of her eyes as the last line of the song swirled around them.

Caught in the midst of fantasies he decided long ago had no place in his life, Mike only half heard the musical warning of letting someone love him before it was too late.

Four

His fingers moved lightly up and down her spine like a classical musician teasing notes from a grand piano. Denise stared up into his eyes. Green clashed with blue in a silent challenge. One dark eyebrow lifted as his right hand skimmed over her flesh. She shivered. He noticed. In her own best interests, she knew she should move away. End this so-called dance now. While she still had the strength to stand. But she didn't. Even when the last of the song had faded away, they stood locked together on the dance floor, each of them somehow reluctant to step back. Away.

But the spell was broken in the next instant when a swell of pounding, driving rock music poured over the crowd. Someone bumped into her from behind, sending her crashing into Mike's chest. He stiffened, grabbed her shoulders to steady her, then immediately released her again.

A shutter dropped over those brilliant green eyes, hiding whatever he was thinking. Feeling. Denise staggered backward a step or two. She winced at the assault of sound blasting into the room. Her head began to pound in time with the pulsing drumbeat.

Looking up at Mike again, she found him glaring at her. What did *he* have to be mad about?

"Come on," he said abruptly, over the music. "I'll take you home."

Home. Yes, she needed to be home. In the quiet safety of her condo, where she could forget all about this night and the almost overpowering sensations she had experienced in Mike's arms.

She turned blindly toward the table where she had left her bag. She felt, rather than heard Mike following close behind. Without a word, she grabbed her purse, Mike snatched up their helmets and with his free hand, steered her to the front door.

The short ride back to her condo was torture.

Denise did everything she could to avoid leaning into Mike's back. She held herself stiffly, her thighs ached with the effort to keep from aligning themselves along his legs. The powerful engine beneath her vibrated with each grumbling roar it sent into the night and every nerve in her body throbbed in response.

Mike guided the bike to a stop in front of her house, then cut the engine. Silence dropped on them like a heavy, uncomfortable blanket. Denise scooted back on the seat. Mike stood up, allowing her to get off the motorcycle with one quick, clumsy move.

She took off the helmet and handed it to him. "Thanks," she said in what she hoped was a light, casual tone. "It was an interesting evening."

He shot her a long, thoughtful look before swinging his left leg over the bike.

"*Interesting,*" he repeated as he pulled his helmet off and set it down on the bike's seat. "That's a good word for it, I guess." He reached down, unhooked a compartment at the back of the motorcycle and reached inside. Pulling out a grocery bag, he stuffed it under his arm, slammed the compartment closed again, then turned to face her. His expression was ferocious.

"Are those my things?" she asked, glancing at the bag.

"Yeah." He took her elbow in a firm grip, turned her around and started for the front door.

"You know, you don't have to walk me to my porch." She glanced at the front of the condo. The light she had left burning sifted through the bougainvillea vines stretched across the trellis that shadowed her porch. "I'm perfectly safe." At least, she thought, she *would* be safe as soon as he left.

"Humor me," he said, and kept walking.

Short of digging in her heels and screaming for help, she really didn't have much choice.

On the porch, he turned and handed her the rolled-up grocery bag. She glanced down at it, then lifted her gaze to his. Green eyes glittered in the glow of the porch light. A muscle in his jaw twitched. Not exactly the picture of a happy man.

Well, the evening hadn't been a picnic for her, either. But he didn't have to be so obvious about his displeasure. A little polite lying never hurt anybody. Refusing to be intimidated by his biker scowl, Denise forced a smile and said, "Thanks again."

His jaw muscle twitched again and she deliberately looked away to fish in her purse for her key. When she had it, Mike took it from her, opened the door, then gave the key back to her.

Curling her fingers around it, Denise took a step toward safety. "It was a lovely evening," she lied in as convincing a manner as she could manage.

"Don't do that."

She stopped cold and looked up at him. "What?"

"Don't give me the standard good-night speech. It wasn't a lovely evening and you damn well know it."

He glared at her, daring her to contradict him.

"Fine. It wasn't lovely." She nodded abruptly. "Like I said before, it was interesting."

"Oh," he countered quickly, "it was more than that."

She looked at him. "What do you mean?"

"You know what I'm talking about, Denise." He placed one hand on the doorjamb and leaned in close to her.

Too close. She could hardly draw a breath. Yes, she knew what he was talking about, but she would be blasted if she was going to stand there and admit that every time he touched her, her body lit up like a nuclear power plant. "Look Mike, let's just call it a night, all right?"

"Not yet."

Her back flat against the wall, she looked up into eyes that seemed to devour her. A white-hot thread of awareness began to uncoil in the pit of her stomach. Her mouth dry, she muttered thickly, "This is crazy."

"Crazy?" He nodded slowly. "Maybe. But before I go, I intend to do something I've been thinking about all night."

Her heartbeat staggered, stopped, then started again. Slower. Harder. She held her breath as he bent his head toward hers. One kiss. How much trouble could one kiss cause?

The moment his lips met hers though, she knew. This wasn't just a kiss. This was an invasion.

His mouth came down on hers with a raw hunger she had never experienced before. Brilliant light exploded within her in a sunburst of color and sensation. He parted her lips with his tongue, sweeping into her warmth with a plundering confidence that stole her breath and urged her to surrender to the wildness building between them.

Pulling her to him, Mike's hands moved up and down her bare back. Not with the gentle, teasing caresses he had shown her at O'Doul's, but with urgent, desperate strokes.

Mike arched into her. Need shimmered through her. In one dark corner of her mind, she realized that she was spinning out of control, but she didn't care. She wanted to be closer to him. To feel his lean, muscular form pressed to her.

His belt buckle dug into her abdomen. He widened his stance. Pulled her tightly to him and tore his lips from her mouth to follow the line of her throat. One big hand cupped her behind, holding her hips to his. She felt the hard strength of him and an answering need spiraled to her center.

Tilting her head back, she stared blindly at the light overhead as Mike's mouth and hands tormented her. Her fingers curled into the black leather of his jacket and she felt his muscles tighten and bunch beneath her hands.

Insane. This whole situation was insane. A man she barely knew, causing such passion and desire to swirl through her bloodstream?

From somewhere down the street, the high-pitched yapping of Mrs. Olsen's Yorkie drifted to her.

Gasping for air, Denise realized that she was standing on her front porch, under the telling glow of a seventy-five-watt bulb, letting a man make violent love to her in full view of her neighbors. Any minute now, Mrs. Olsen would be walking past her condo and who knew how many others of her neighbors were glued to their front windows peering out from behind their draperies? She had to stop him, she knew. This couldn't happen. She couldn't allow either of them to take this one step further.

Then he slipped one hand beneath the fabric of her dress and smoothed his fingertips over the curve of her behind. A harsh moan erupted from the back of her throat and her thoughts dissolved under the onslaught of fiery emotions.

As if her sigh of surrender had been a bucket of cold water tossed at his head, Mike stopped suddenly and lifted his head. Trembling, she met his gaze and knew the confusion she saw there was mirrored in her own.

Viciously, he rubbed the back of his neck with one hand, took a step back from her and drew a long, shaky breath.

"Denise..."

She held one hand up for silence. Shaking her head like a sleepwalker finally waking up, she said, "Let it go, all right? I'm not up to a discussion right now."

"Yeah, me either."

Breathe in, breathe out. Simple really, once you got the hang of it. After practicing a few more times, Denise forced herself to move for the door. Once over the threshold, half hidden behind the safety of her solid oak door, she looked at him and said simply, "Good night, Mike."

He nodded, then turned, hurrying down the flower-lined walk toward the street. A moment later, the Harley roared into life and carried him away.

Usually, working on motorcycles brought him peace. With his hands and mind busy, he didn't have the time or energy to worry about anything else. Sometimes, it was enough just to walk into the service bay behind his shop. The rock music playing on the radio, the easy conversation between the mechanics, even the cool ocean breeze that blew through the two open ends of the workshop, all worked together to make Mike Ryan a happy man.

Until today.

For the third time in as many minutes, Mike tried to fit the wrench head around a stubborn nut. He swore disgustedly as the wrench slipped off target for the third time, this time skinning his knuckles.

"Damn!"

"Bad day, Mike?"

He didn't even bother to look at his chief mechanic, Bob Dolan. The nosy man had been hinting for information all day. "Butt out, Bob."

"Nothin' to me, of course," the other man said from the workbench on the far side of the service bay. "But if I was in a foul mood because of some woman, I'd just forget about her and move on."

Mike smiled to himself. "So speaks the man married for twenty-seven years."

Bob laughed. "True, but only because she hasn't made me mad, yet. For instance, you don't see me grumbling at everyone who comes near me, do ya?"

Mike set the wrench down, put both hands at the small of his back and stretched. Every muscle in his body ached with fatigue. No sleep and a day of frustration was liable to do that to a man. He shouldn't even have bothered going in to work today, he told himself. It wasn't like anyone there needed his help. He had the best bike mechanics in the state working for him. And Bob's wife Tina handled the customers in the showroom better than he ever had.

But it had been a matter of principle. He didn't want to admit that thoughts of Denise Torrance would ruin his day as effectively as they had ruined his night.

His plan hadn't worked. Instead, he had spent the last eight hours grumbling, complaining and pushing his employees until it was a wonder they all hadn't quit in protest.

"So," Bob asked gently, "you feel like talking about it now?"

He glanced at the other man and shrugged. "Nothing to talk about."

Shaking his head, Bob set the carburetor he was rebuilding down on the bench, then walked across the room to stand beside his boss. He tossed a quick look over his shoulder at the two other mechanics working thirty feet away before saying, "Spit it out, Mike. Something's been eating at you all day."

Mike wiped his greasy hands on an even greasier rag. He never should have hired a man who knew him as well as Bob Dolan did. Ever since they were in the service together, Bob had had the unnerving ability to read Mike's mind.

"It'd be different if you were the kind to suffer in silence," the man continued. "But whatever it is that's bothering you keeps spilling over onto the rest of us."

Pointless to argue. Giving him a rueful smile Mike said, "Sorry. I guess I have been taking it out on you guys."

Two bushy eyebrows arched high on the other man's forehead. Bob scratched his salt-and-pepper beard, then folded massive arms across a barrel chest. "So, Ryan, what's her name?"

Mike shot him a look. "Who says it's a woman?"

The mechanic snorted a laugh. "What else *could* it be?"

Disgusted with himself, Mike nodded. "True." He looked at his oldest friend, silently debating whether or not to ask for advice. It wasn't as if he were going to be seeing Denise again. So technically, he didn't really *need* advice. On the other hand, it might be good to talk about this woman and the effect she had had on him.

Besides, he and Bob had served in the marines together. They'd been in and out of more rough spots than most people dream about. And Bob Dolan was the one friend Mike had allowed himself to keep when he finally decided to leave the corps.

Knowing it was inevitable anyway, he said, "Her name's Denise."

"Ah…" Bob grinned, wiggled his eyebrows and waited.

"There is no 'Ah' here, Dolan," Mike warned him.

"Hell, it's high time you found an Ah, Ryan."

"I'm not interested in an Ah, Dolan. Besides, I didn't find her," Mike argued. "I kind of… stumbled onto her."

"Even better."

Mike scowled at his best friend. Not many people would guess that behind Bob's hard, dangerous-looking biker exterior beat the heart of a true romantic. For years, Dolan had been trying to convince Mike to find a woman and settle down. "I knew it was a mistake to talk to you about her."

"All right, all right," Bob said, wiping any trace of interest from his features. "I won't say another word about how you need someone. Not even about how you're not getting any younger—despite the ponytail.''

Mike's teeth ground together.

"Go ahead, tell me," his friend urged, not even bothering to disguise his curiosity.

"There's not much to tell." Mike squinted at the late afternoon sunshine filling the far end of the service bay. Actually, there was plenty to tell. But he had never been the locker-room-storyteller kind of guy.

"She's an accountant," he finally said.

"Oh." Bob sounded disappointed.

Mike laughed and the two other mechanics turned to look at him before going back to their work.

"I know what you're thinking," he told his friend. "But she doesn't look like any accountant you've ever seen."

"Oh?" Interested again.

"She's smart, she's funny. Independent as hell." He shot his friend a quick look. "She punched me on the chin."

"She *is* smart."

"Funny." Mike shook his head slowly. "I don't know what it is about her, but something…"

"Good, good," Bob grinned. "A woman you don't have figured out from the first minute you meet her."

"Maybe that's it," he muttered, more to himself than his friend. "Well, that and a good old-fashioned case of lust."

"You think so, huh?" Bob asked. "Sounds to me like something more."

"Well, it isn't." Mike turned his back on the other man and picked up the wrench again. All right, he was willing to admit that kissing her had been like nothing he had ever felt before. He was even willing to admit that he admired her. She had climbed on board his motorcycle despite her reluctance. And she played a surprisingly good game of pool. For a novice. Immediately, the memory of leaning over her, his body pressed to hers while he helped her line up a shot came to him. He smothered a groan and closed his eyes. Her image remained in the front of his mind and his body tightened uncomfortably.

No good, he told himself. She was no one-night stand and he wasn't interested in anything else. Abruptly, Mike slammed the wrench down onto the workbench and turned for the rear of the service bay where he kept his bike parked.

Only one way to handle this, he told himself. He and Denise had to talk. He had to let her know that whatever it was between them wasn't going to get the chance to grow. He wouldn't allow it.

"Where you goin'?" Bob called out.

"To set a few things straight," Mike answered.

As the Harley roared off into the late afternoon, Bob Dolan rubbed his palms together gleefully. Then he walked to the showroom to tell his wife about the woman who was going to bring down Mike Ryan.

Five

Denise stepped into her father's office and waited while he finished his phone conversation. He glanced at her briefly, waved her inside, then turned his gaze to the sheaf of papers on his desk.

Through the bank of floor-to-ceiling windows behind him, she watched the afternoon sun dipping toward the ocean. Streaks of clouds along the horizon gleamed with pale, rich color.

Color that was lacking in the large office's decor. Soft, cream walls surrounded what looked like an acre of sand-colored carpeting. Richard Torrance's mammoth mahogany desk sat squarely in the center of the room, facing the door. He kept his back to a spectacular view in favor of keeping his mind on the sheets of facts and figures that were always in front of him.

Four guest chairs sat clustered on the visitor's side of the desk and on one wall was a small, tasteful bar and two maroon leather sofas. No filing cabinets, adding machines or computers could be found in the roomy office. Those were relegated to an anteroom behind a narrow door to one side of the bar.

No clutter. In his office or his life. Richard Torrance preferred order. Indeed, insisted on it.

When he hung up the receiver, he didn't look up, but went on making notations in the file before him.

"I'm going home now," Denise said softly, not really expecting a response, but waiting for it anyway.

He finished scribbling notes to himself as she watched him. A tall man, even seated he was an imposing figure. Light brown hair dusted with gray at the temples, he had a narrow, thoughtful face and sharp, pale blue eyes that rarely missed a thing.

"Hmmm?" Richard Torrance looked up from the file he was scanning. He glanced at the clock mounted on the wall opposite his desk, then frowned at his daughter. "Early, isn't it?"

"Only fifteen minutes or so," she said. Digging into her purse, she rummaged in its depths for her antacid bottle. When she had it, she pulled it out, took two of the tablets and popped them into her mouth. Slowly, she chewed and the familiar, chalky fruit flavor filled her mouth. Dropping the bottle back into her purse, she waited.

"Is there a problem?" her father asked.

A problem? she thought. Yes, but nothing he would care to hear about. She could just imagine her father's reaction to the knowledge that she had actually gone to O'Doul's—with a biker, no less.

Visions of Mike Ryan leapt to mind as they had all last night. She had tossed and turned restlessly, her body still humming with the sexual fire he had stoked and then abandoned. And while her body burned, her mind had raged at her. How could she have let herself be swept away by something as unpredictable as *hormones?*

She looked at her father and not for the first time, wished that she could talk to him. *Really* talk to him.

"Well?" Richard prompted. "Something here at work? Something I should know about?" She didn't answer right away, so he went on. "Did you finish the Smithson file? He'll be here at eight o'clock sharp tomorrow morning."

She wasn't even surprised that her father assumed whatever was bothering her concerned work. To Richard Torrance, his accounting firm was the most important thing in the world. In dedicating himself to its success, he had neglected his wife and overlooked his daughter—until that daughter was of an age to take her rightful place in the firm.

"Denise?" he repeated. "The Smithson file?"

"It's finished."

He gave her one of his rare smiles. "If your work is up to date, what could be the problem?"

What indeed? She couldn't tell him the truth. He would never understand her fascination with Mike. Even *she* didn't understand it.

As she mentally groped for something to say, the telephone on his desk rang and saved her.

Her father lifted the receiver. "Hello? Hello, Thomas," he said, dismissing Denise with an absent nod. He swiveled his chair around so that he could stare out the window behind his desk at the ocean beyond, while he talked.

Denise waited another moment or two before quietly slipping out. She wasn't sure if she should be relieved or hurt that he had already forgotten about her.

Mike felt it again. The sense that worried eyes were watching him as he steered the motorcycle up to Denise's condo. Nudging the kickstand into place, he stood up, swung his leg over the bike and pulled off his helmet.

Glancing around the quiet, moneyed street, he noted the immaculate lawns, the well-cared-for homes and shuddered in response. What the hell was *he* doing in a tidy, self-satisfied neighborhood like this? He had spent most of his life avoiding little splotches of domesticity and yet here he was, riding up to a neat little condo to talk to a woman who could mean nothing but trouble for him.

The woman who had, with one kiss, made him forget everything but her. All of his rules, all of his plans had come to nothing once he had tasted Denise Torrance's mouth.

Which brought him to why he was back, now.

He had to face her. Tell her in no uncertain terms that it would be best if they just stayed away from each other. He had thought it all out. There was no other answer. Denise was the house-in-the-suburbs kind of woman—and Mike got cold chills just *thinking* about settling down.

Great chemistry or not—this was going nowhere.

Leaving his bike parked on the street, he carried his helmet with him as he marched up the front walk.

Denise watched him approach the house and every nerve in her body went on red alert. Why had he come back? Why hadn't he just stayed away?

She glanced down at herself and groaned. Faded, baggy gym shorts and an old, oversize T-shirt with a picture of Tweety Bird on it did *not* make for an impressive outfit.

The doorbell rang and her stomach pitched.

She took a moment to collect herself, then turned the knob and opened the door.

Her gaze locked with his. All day she had been telling herself that whatever she had felt for him had been a momentary aberration. A lightninglike flash of desire caused by the excitement of the moment.

Lies. All lies.

Instantly the same, illogical, overpowering stirrings of desire rose inside her again. Her gaze slipped over him quickly, thoroughly. The tight black T-shirt, straining over his muscular shoulders and chest. The worn Levis that hugged his long legs in a soft, faded grip.

"We have to talk," he said, his voice rough.

Talk. Denise drew in a long, shaky breath and told herself to get a grip. There was nothing sexual about *talking*. Besides, she was twenty-nine years old. Too darned old to let her hormones be her guide. She could do this. She was an *accountant* for Pete's sake. Accountants were not the stuff of wild, sexy fantasies starring muscular, dangerous-looking bikers.

To prove to herself that there was nothing to be worried about, she pulled the door wider and said, "Come in."

He stepped past her in the narrow entryway and a whiff of Old Spice staggered her. Frantically, she started to mentally recite the multiplication tables. Starting at the two's. Numbers. Numbers she was comfortable with. Numbers she understood. Numbers were her only hope.

Closing the front door, Denise moved around him in as wide a circle as she could manage and led the way into the living room. Her gaze moved quickly over the familiar, spartan room. White walls, blue carpet. A sofa and two wing chairs upholstered in a dark blue fabric with bright red-and-yellow throw pillows for splashes of color.

On the low coffee table were a stack of files from the office and a rapidly cooling cup of herbal tea. The TV was on, turned to the news, but the sound was so low as to be only a small hum of voices in the background.

Curling her toes into the thick carpet, she turned to face him. Mentally, she was up to the five's. He looked out of place. Uncomfortable.

"Denise," he began, "what happened last night…"

Multiplication abandoned, she broke in hurriedly.

"Can't happen again. For heaven's sake, Mike. We have nothing in common."

"Agreed," he said, exhaling on a rush of relieved breath. Half smiling, he added, "You're not exactly my type."

"And you're not the kind of man I would feel comfortable taking to a company dinner."

He shuddered at the thought.

Good, she told herself. They were making progress now. Obviously, he had been doing a lot of thinking about this, too. And apparently, he had reached the very same conclusions. No matter how exciting...how *tempting* a relationship with him might be, it simply couldn't happen.

There was no future in it and she refused to set herself up for a broken heart.

"So we understand each other?" Mike said and took a step closer.

"Of course," her mouth went dry as she moved toward him. Her heart pounded against her rib cage and her blood thundered in her ears.

"You and I have no business even *thinking* about being together."

"Absolutely not." The whole idea was ridiculous.

"I'm not interested in love or anything else that comes tied up in a neat little package," Mike grumbled. His gaze moved over her hotly and she shivered in response.

"I don't believe in quick little affairs." She wanted what she had always wanted. Someone to love. Someone to love her.

"Exactly," he muttered thickly and reached out

to smooth her hair back from her face. "It doesn't matter a damn what you do to me."

"Or what you do to me." She inhaled sharply as his fingertips brushed across her cheek. Jagged streaks of heat shot through her body. "Hormones," she whispered.

"Lust," he said softly, urgently.

"Pure and simple. That's all it *could* be." She tilted her head back to keep her gaze locked with his. "Right?"

"Right. Good, old-fashioned lust."

She took a deep, unsteady breath and dragged the scent of Old Spice deep into her lungs.

"Oh," she said on a sigh, "we're in trouble, aren't we?"

"Damn straight," he said and brought his mouth down on hers.

She wrapped her arms around his neck, pulling him closer. Her lips parted for him and her tongue met his stroke for stroke. In a wild, desperate joining, their mouths mated, breath mingling, tongues exploring, caressing.

Denise arched into him, brushing her rigid nipples across his broad chest. She sucked in a gasp of air that shot from her lungs as one of Mike's hands slipped beneath the waistband of her shorts. His fingertips lifted the band of her bikini panties and his hand dipped lower, to caress her bare behind. She moved into him and felt his body, already hard and eager.

Desperately, hungrily, his tongue moved in and out of her mouth, touching, tasting. This was no tender, romantic coupling. This was need. A deep, instinctive need that demanded completion. He held her mouth with his as if trying to claim her breath for his own. She met his urgency with a wild, overwhelming passion that threatened to leave her puddled on the floor. When he finally tore his mouth from hers, Denise almost moaned at the loss.

But a moment later, he was tugging her T-shirt up and over her head and she was helping him. His palms cupped her breasts and his thumbs gently stroked the hard, sensitive tips of her nipples. She groaned in the back of her throat and began tearing at his shirt, pulling it free of his jeans.

In as frantic a state as she was, Mike released her long enough to yank the shirt off and throw it to the floor. Then he grabbed her again and pulled her tight against him. Flesh to flesh, heat to heat, the fire already raging between them burst into an inferno of passion.

With his knee, Mike shoved the coffee table out of the way. Absently, Denise heard the crash as the table tilted and fell on its side. Her teacup clattered quietly but she didn't care. He sank to the rug, dragging her with him, all the while, touching and teasing every inch of her body.

She reached for him and held on to his shoulders, reveling in the feel of his muscled flesh beneath her hands. Warm, strong, his tanned chest lightly sprinkled with dark, curly hair, he looked wonderful.

"Denise," he whispered before bending his head to take one of her nipples into his mouth. His lips and teeth worked the tender flesh until she was writhing beneath him, helplessly caught in the net of desire they had blindly stumbled into.

Denise pulled the rubber band from his ponytail and tangled her fingers in this thick, black hair. She felt his right hand sweep down her body to drag her shorts and panties off and she lifted her hips to assist him.

"Now, Mike," she pleaded in an agonized whisper. "Hurry. I have to feel you inside me, Mike. I need..." Her voice faded into silence. How could she possibly explain what she needed when she hardly understood it herself? This was more than desire. More than lust. Something within her was clamoring to be a part of him. To feel him slide his body into hers. She had never known such hunger, such mindless need before.

It both excited and terrified her.

"Soon, honey," he promised and moved away from her, despite the groan erupting from her chest. In seconds he had disposed of not only her clothes, but his. Then he was back, kneeling between her thighs, kneading the flesh of her behind with his strong hands. She twisted in his grip, reaching for him.

"Mike," she whispered. "Please Mike, now."

"Now," he promised in a hushed voice and lifted her hips for his entry.

Mike looked down at her as he pushed himself deeply inside her tight, hot body. She arched into him and a broken cry tore from her throat as he filled her. He clenched his teeth tight to bite back a groan of satisfaction building in his own chest. He held perfectly still, buried inside her, fighting for control. An explosive climax was only a breath away and he would be damned if he would give in to the pleasure before she was ready to take that leap with him.

In the space of a few heartbeats, he was able to move within her again. And then there was nothing but the overpowering, driving urge to brand her as his. To fill her so deeply, so completely, that even when they weren't together, he would still be a part of her.

She lifted her legs and locked them around his hips, drawing him tighter, closer.

Mike looked down into her blue eyes and saw the stunned wonder he knew was written on his own features. He pressed his mouth to hers and their bodies raced toward completion. He swallowed her cries when they were at last swept over the edge of passion and fell tumbling into peace.

When it was over, they lay locked together, neither of them willing—or able—to move, to separate. Heart pounding, Mike rolled over onto his back, keeping her with him, cradling her close. Her head on his chest, he felt her breath brush across his skin and tried to get feeling back into his limbs.

Now that his body had found rest though, his mind finally kicked into gear. As one, undeniable fact presented itself, he had to bite back a groan of disgust. He had acted like some dumb teenager. For the first time in years, he had acted without thinking. As a result, the two of them might now be in deeper trouble than either of them had thought.

She lifted her head and looked down at him. Giving him a rueful smile, Denise said, "Well, so much for talking."

Reluctantly, he smiled back at her. Damn. Now what? Obviously, the realization that had occurred to him hadn't popped into her mind yet.

"Denise," he said, then paused, hoping for inspiration.

"I know," she mumbled.

"What the hell happened?" Stupid question, he told himself. He knew damn well what had happened. For the first time in years, he had allowed his body to make his decisions for him.

"*That* I don't know," she said, snuggling against him.

He ran the flat of his hand down her spine, wondering just how he should say what he had to say.

Across the room from them, the telephone rang. Neither of them glanced at it. On the second ring, the answering machine picked up. Seconds later, Denise heard her father's commanding voice. "Denise? Apparently, you're not at home."

She lifted her head and shot a covert, almost guilty look at the phone.

Mike watched her expression shift and change as she quickly scooted off and away from him. He frowned thoughtfully as the voice on the machine continued.

"I hope that means you're thoroughly prepared for the Smithson meeting tomorrow. And don't forget you're having lunch with Pete Donahue from Donahue's Delights. My secretary's made an appointment for you at the Tidewater for twelve o'clock. Since he's a new client, I'll expect you to impress on him just what Torrance Accounting can do for his business.''

Denise groped around on the floor for her shirt and shorts. Still keeping one eye on her, Mike snatched up his own clothes and got dressed. Amazing, he thought as he looked at her. A moment ago, she had been cuddled naked against him and now she was acting as though nothing had happened.

"So," her father continued, apparently unconcerned about taking up her entire message tape. "What was this problem, you said you had?"

She shot a surprised look at the machine.

Mike's eyebrows lifted. Problem?

"Well," Richard said and sighed heavily. "No point in asking this infernal machine what's going on. You can tell me tomorrow...I'll pencil you in for 3:10 in the afternoon. Goodbye."

Real friendly guy, he thought. The man talked to his own daughter as if she were a client.

"You need an appointment to talk to your father?" Mike asked.

"He's a busy man." She stood up and bent to right the table. Mike helped her, then gathered the fallen file papers while she picked up the broken teacup.

Her features were tight. There was no sign of the wild, passionate woman of a few moments before. Odd, how just the sound of her father's voice could do that to her.

Odder still, that it mattered to him.

"Lunch with Donahue's Delights, huh?" He tried

a smile on her, but there was no reaction. "They make great frozen burritos."

She nodded and folded her arms across her chest in an unconscious symbol of self-defense. What the hell was going on here? And why had she just clammed up on him when a while ago she had nearly burned his skin off?

But maybe it was better this way. Once he said what he had to say, the atmosphere in the room was certain to get a little chilly, anyway.

"Denise, about what just happened..."

"Let's not *talk* again, okay?"

"Dammit, we have to talk." Now was not the time to shut herself off from him. Fifteen minutes ago, maybe. But not now.

"It was stupid. What else is there to say?"

"Plenty." He reached up and pushed his hair back from his face with both hands. "It wasn't just stupid. It was irresponsible. We didn't use any protection, Denise."

Six

Was the world spinning? Or was it just this one room?

Suddenly sick to her stomach, Denise blinked furiously, trying to get her vision to clear. It wasn't working.

She clapped one hand to her mouth and looked at him through wide eyes. Protection. Birth control. Good heavens. This kind of thing only happened in bad movies. How could they have forgotten something so basic? Because, she admitted silently, they had been too busy dealing with something far more basic.

"Oh, Lord."

Plopping down onto the couch, she propped her elbows on her knees and cupped her face in her hands.

He paced back and forth in front of the couch in long, hurried strides. "As far as one worry goes," he said in a self-disgusted tone, "I can tell you that I'm healthy."

She was even more stupid than she had at first thought. She hadn't even *considered* that particular aspect of life in modern times.

"Me, too," she said when she noticed that he had stopped pacing to look at her questioningly. Why wouldn't she be? At twenty-nine, she had had exactly two lovers. Including Mike. No wonder she had messed things up so badly. She didn't have nearly enough experience to be able to deal with a man like Mike Ryan.

She swallowed a groan and tried to quiet her mind so she could hear him.

"As far as a pregnancy goes, though..." He stopped pacing again suddenly and she felt him looking at her. Slowly, she lifted her head to meet his gaze. "Please tell me you're on the Pill," Mike said grimly.

"All right," Denise obliged him wearily. "I'm on the Pill.

"No, you're not."

"No," she said and this time her groan wouldn't be silenced. "I'm not."

"Perfect."

She glared at him. Was he trying to lay the blame for this...incident entirely at *her* feet? Well, he could forget that idea right now. It took two people to do what they had just done.

Two very stupid people.

"I'm very sorry I wasn't more prepared," she snapped and tried to ignore the curl of worry already taking shape in the pit of her stomach. She only hoped that was *all* that was taking shape.

"That's not what I meant."

"Of course it is." She jumped to her feet and walked past him, heading for the kitchen. It didn't surprise her in the least to hear him following her.

She marched straight to the refrigerator and opened it. Reaching inside for a bottle of water, she grabbed two automatically and handed him one as she closed the door again.

The perfect hostess, her mind laughed at her.

Mike twisted the top off, lifted the bottle and drained half of it immediately.

Denise settled for a long sip before saying hotly, "This must be a new world's record. Not just for you, personally. But for *all* men."

"What are you talking about?"

She shook her head at him. "The sheets, so to speak, have hardly cooled off and already you're trying to weasle your way out of any responsibility for possibly conceiving a child."

"Hold on a minute," he said and stood up straight.

"You were there too, Mike. You could have stopped. You could have used something. Don't try to turn everything around and make this all *my* fault."

"That's not what I said," he argued. "And honey, I don't weasle out of responsibility. All I said was, I wish you had been taking the Pill." He leaned one hip against the slate blue countertop and looked at her.

"Well, so do I," she countered. "And stop calling me honey."

He drained the rest of his ice water, set the bottle on the countertop behind him and said deliberately, "So *honey*, why *aren't* you on the Pill?"

She scowled at him. "Not that it's any of your business, but they make me sick."

"What?"

"Birth control pills. They make me sick."

"Wonderful."

She stiffened, took another drink and said, "I don't do this sort of thing every day, you know." No, she thought. More like once in the last six years. "There hasn't been a real big need for regular birth control in my life."

Mike folded his arms across his broad chest defensively and looked at her for a long minute. "This isn't getting us anywhere. What's done is done. But isn't there something you can do—after the fact?"

A short, strangled laugh shot from her throat before she could stop it. "Sure," she said, sarcasm dripping off every word. "I could bury the warts of a toad under an oak tree by the light of a full moon."

He frowned at her, but she went on, warming to her theme. "Or, how about I boil up a little eye of newt and drink it down while balancing on one foot?"

"Denise..."

Patience gone, she slammed her half-full water

bottle down onto the counter. Liquid sloshed up the neck and spilled onto her hand. She wiped it dry on her shorts and snapped, "Just go, Mike. Get out." Storming through the kitchen back to the living room, she felt her own fears fade away in the face of her anger.

It was as though she were stuck in a bad soap opera with a lousy script. Bad boy takes advantage of good girl, then accuses her of trying to trap him. Even as she thought it though, she had to admit that he hadn't taken advantage of her. It had been a mutual seduction. Incredibly careless, but mutual.

Unfortunately, *she* would be the only one to pay the price if Mother Nature presented a bill.

"Dammit, Denise," he shouted and grabbed her arm to turn her around to face him. "Stop treating me like I'm public enemy number one just because I don't want you to be pregnant."

She yanked free of him. "I'm not mad about that," she told him. "I'm angry because you only bothered to be concerned about it *afterward.*"

"Neither one of us was doing much thinking." He moved in close to her.

She didn't want to be reminded. She didn't want to have to think about why she had reacted to him—responded to him as she had. It had never happened before. She had never known such an all-consuming need to be with a man. Until she had met Mike Ryan, Denise's love life had been as boring as the rest of her life.

Boring, her mind chided her. But safe.

"Denise," he went on, "if we made a mistake, we made it together."

Mistake. What they had done was foolish. Irresponsible. But a mistake? Instantly, she remembered the sense of completion she had experienced when he entered her. When his body and hers were joined.

Was finding that magic a mistake?

And if they had conceived a child—would the child be a mistake as well? She flinched from that notion.

"How long until we know?" he asked, his voice quiet.

For a moment, she wasn't sure what he was talking about. Then it dawned on her. She glanced up at him. "*I'll* know for sure one way or the other in about ten days."

He nodded. "Okay. So let's not make ourselves crazy about this yet."

That seemed reasonable, she thought and felt some of the tension drain from her.

"If there *is* a baby..." He paused. "Hell, we'll have plenty of time to figure out what's next."

"*We?*" She looked up at him.

"Yeah. *We.*" His green eyes locked with hers. She couldn't have looked away if she had tried "I told you already, Denise. I don't weasle out of my responsibilities."

A speech designed to warm any girl's heart.

"I think you'd better leave now," she said quietly.

Seconds ticked past.

She sat down on the couch, drew her knees up to

her chest and wrapped her arms around them. She kept her gaze determinedly away from his.

"Fine," he said after a while, just as quietly. "I'll go. For now. But I'll be back."

She listened to the sounds of his footsteps as he moved through the condo. After the front door had closed behind him, she let her head fall backward against the couch. She closed her eyes and told herself that he had been right about one thing. It was too early to worry. She would find out soon enough if there was a need for it. And then, she would have nine long months to do all the worrying she wanted.

By the time her lunch appointment rolled around the next day, Denise had convinced herself that everything would be fine. After all, most couples had to try for years before conceiving a child. What were the odds she and Mike Ryan could accomplish such a feat with one, mind-boggling lovemaking session?

Astronomical.

In numbers, she told herself, there was comfort.

Pete Donahue sent her a smile as she signed the check for lunch and slipped her Visa card back into her purse. A widower, Pete was nice, fairly attractive and financially secure. And a week ago, she might have been flattered by his obvious interest in her.

Unfortunately today, she looked at his thinning blond hair and saw it as thick and black. His calm gray eyes were no substitute for the memory of the deep green eyes that had haunted her sleep. And, she admitted, blue suits just didn't have the same fascination for her as tight black T-shirts.

"You can tell your father that I'm happy with Torrance Accounting," Pete said, smiling. "Maybe then he can relax."

"My father? Relax?" Denise grabbed her purse and stood up. She maneuvered her way through the maze of tables in the crowded restaurant, then turned and waited for him to join her in the entryway.

Pete chuckled as he stepped past her to open the front door for her. "I used to be like him, you know. So wrapped up in business that I couldn't see beyond my own nose."

"What happened?" she asked idly and walked into brilliant afternoon sunshine.

"My wife died."

Denise looked at him quickly, lifting one hand to shade her eyes. "I'm sorry."

"It was several years ago," he said, holding one hand up to assure her that he wasn't wounded. "But her death did make me realize that life was too short to miss it all because of business appointments."

Her father, unfortunately, had never learned that lesson. When her mother died, Denise was only eleven. Unlike Pete Donahue, Richard Torrance had buried himself even deeper in his work once there was no one around to demand a slice of his time.

No one but a little girl.

And that girl had spent the past eighteen years trying to make Daddy proud of her. Was he? she wondered. Had any of her accomplishments been enough to get Richard Torrance's attention?

"Thanks for lunch, Denise."

"Hmmm? Oh," she said, as he walked her to her car. "My pleasure."

The hot summer sun bounced off the asphalt and tossed heat at them like heavy stones.

"I don't suppose I could interest you in the ballet Friday night?"

Caught off guard, she stalled, searching for something to say. "Uh..." She couldn't afford to offend her father's newest client. On the other hand, the only man she was interested in at the moment was someone she was working hard to forget.

"Maybe not," Pete said for her. "Somehow, I think he'd object."

She looked up at him and he jerked his head in the direction of her car.

There, propped casually against the right front fender, was Mike Ryan.

Despite her best efforts, her heartbeat accelerated. Her gaze swept over him, taking in the blue jeans, the white T-shirt and the huge Harley parked alongside her car.

He looked like every mother's nightmare.

And every daughter's fantasy.

Even as her blood rushed through her veins, she realized that she would have a much better chance at forgetting all about him if he would just stay away.

As they approached, Mike pushed up from the car and stood, long legs planted in a wide, almost belligerent stance. He looked every inch the dangerous male.

"Hello, Mike," she said.

He nodded abruptly and shifted his gaze to the man beside her.

"Pete Donahue, Mike Ryan," she said. "Mike, Pete Donahue."

Mike took the man's extended hand and gave it a brief, hard shake. "Good burritos."

"Thanks," Pete nodded, flashed Denise a quick smile and asked, "I'll speak to you at the end of the month?"

"That's fine," she told him, grateful that he was leaving so quickly. With Mike still in his Tarzan stance, it was probably a good idea. "I'll call your secretary."

He lifted one hand in a halfhearted wave and walked off to his own car.

A heartbeat later, she whirled around to face Mike Ryan. "What are you doing here?" she demanded, squinting up at him.

"I needed to see you," he said.

"So you show up at my business lunch?"

"Your lunch was over."

"That's not the point."

"No," he muttered thickly, "the point is, that I can't get you out of my mind."

She sucked in a gulp of air and told herself that it didn't mean anything. Obviously, they were both being plagued with some weird sort of attraction that they were just going to have to deal with sensibly.

"This is nuts," she whispered.

"Among other things," he agreed.

Mike looked down at her and felt something inside him shift, soften. Damn, this was playing with fire. For years, he had managed to avoid feeling anything more than a passing fondness for any woman.

He didn't want love. He didn't want to *need* anyone.

Yet, here he was, chasing after the one woman who could be real trouble for him. Denise touched him in ways he didn't even understand. Despite her strength, there was a vulnerability to her that brought all of his protective instincts rushing to the surface.

A moment ago, he had wanted to slam his fist into Pete Donahue's face simply because the man had been able to make Denise smile. He had the insane desire to stake a claim on her. To fight off any intruding males.

Blast it, around her, he wanted to go find some dragons he could slay and lay at her feet. He wasn't sure he liked this feeling, but it was too big to ignore.

Not to mention, he thought with a glimmer of panic, the possibility of a baby.

"Mike," she said, shaking her head.

"I know what you're going to say," he interrupted. "Jeez, I said it myself all last night. We're too different. We have nothing in common."

"Exactly." She took a step closer.

"And it doesn't matter." He moved toward her. "Look, you said we've got about ten days before we know for sure about…"

"Yes," she interrupted.

He swallowed hard past the knot of fear that had been stuck in his throat since the moment he had realized that there *might* be a baby. "All I'm saying is, why don't we spend those ten days together? Give us a chance to get to know each other a little."

She was already shaking her head, so he started talking faster. "If there's a decision to be made, wouldn't it be easier if we could face it together? As friends?"

"Friends?" Denise asked.

"All right," he conceded with a half smile. "Maybe friends is asking too much of either one of us." He rested both hands on her shoulders. Gently, his thumbs kneaded her muscles through the fabric of her red cotton suit. "I'm not talking about forever here, Denise," he said, his voice tight and low. "I'm talking about two grown-ups who share something...incredible."

She stiffened and shot him a quick look. Hell, he knew she would rather hear about hearts and flowers. Declarations of love and promises he had sworn never to make. But if they were going to be together, even if it was only for ten days, then she had to know that he wasn't going to fall in love.

He had seen close up just how love could destroy people.

"I told you before," she said quietly. "I don't do little affairs."

"I'm not asking you to."

"Aren't you?"

He scowled, released her and said, "I don't know what I'm asking for. All I know is that something happened last night." He didn't understand it any better than she did. Could hardly define it. But somehow, when he and Denise had made love, he had felt a sense of *rightness* that he had never known before. It was more than great sex. How *much* more scared the hell out of him. But not enough to make him keep his distance. "There's something between us, Denise."

She shivered.

"I'm not willing to give that up yet," he said flatly. "Are you?"

She looked away from him, staring blindly across the parking lot. He waited what seemed forever for her to finally shift her gaze back to his.

Mike wasn't sure what he would do if she turned him down and sent him away. He held his breath until his chest hurt with the effort.

"No," she admitted. "I want to be, but no. I'm not."

Air rushed from his lungs. He felt himself grinning like a fool as he reached for her hand. "Come with me."

"Where?"

"Just for a ride." He drew her toward his motorcycle.

"I have to get back to work," she said as she dragged her feet.

Mike flicked a quick glance at her and felt his pulse speed up. What was it about this woman? "It's your father's business. Take an extra hour."

At the mention of her father, Denise's expression tightened slightly. "No, I really can't."

He pulled her to him, slipped one arm around her waist and tugged her tight up against his side. Staring down into the wide blue eyes that had kept him awake most of the previous night, he whispered, "One hour. Tell him your lunch went long."

The tip of her tongue smoothed across her bottom lip and Mike's gaze tracked it. A familiar hunger rippled through him.

"All right," she finally said. "But just an hour."

He smiled and Denise's stomach flipped over. Telling herself that she was being a fool where Mike was concerned didn't seem to be helping. She hitched her suit skirt up to midthigh, climbed aboard the narrow seat and pulled on the helmet he handed her.

Mike got on the bike and sat down in front of her. Plopping her purse down onto her lap, she leaned forward and wrapped her arms around his middle.

"Ready?" he called loudly as he fired the engine.

No, she thought, but nodded against his back anyway. The powerful bike lunged forward and in seconds, they were roaring down the Coast Highway.

Four hours later, Mike took her back to her car.

"You're a pretty good pool player," he said.

"I distinctly hear, 'For a girl', in that statement," Denise countered and handed him her helmet.

"Are you accusing me of being a sexist?" He gave her a slow, lopsided grin that set off firecrackers in her bloodstream.

Denise tugged at the lapels of her suit jacket and straightened her short red skirt. "Sexist? Of course not. Male? Definitely."

He chuckled softly. "I'll pick you up at your place at eight."

She checked her wristwatch. Five o'clock. Only three hours to go before she climbed back onto that bike of his and… "Five o'clock!"

"What's the matter?" he asked as she hurried around to the driver's side of her car.

Denise hardly spared him a glance. She fumbled in her purse for the keys. Pulling them free, she opened the car door and threw her purse onto the passenger seat.

"Denise?" he said, louder this time. "What's gong on? What's the big hurry?"

"I had an appointment with my father at 3:10," she reminded him and slid behind the wheel. She fired up the engine, pulled out of the parking lot and sped down the street toward her office.

Most of the cars were gone by the time she arrived. Naturally, her father's was still there. The man never left work before seven at night.

Hurrying into the building, she grabbed the first elevator and rode it impatiently to the third floor. She bolted through the slowly opening doors and hustled down the long, quiet hall to Richard Torrance's office.

She knocked gently and walked in.

He looked up from his desk, gave her a vague smile, then returned his gaze to his work.

"Father, I'm—"

"Going home now?"

"Uh…"

"Fine, fine," her father muttered and began scribbling on the paper in front of him. "See you tomorrow then."

Denise stared at him for a long, thoughtful moment. He didn't remember. Obviously he had forgotten all about their appointment. He must not have written it down after all. Apparently something more important than his daughter had cropped up, wiping all thought of an appointment with her out of his mind. She wondered if he had noticed at all that she hadn't been in the office for most of the day.

The only sound in the room was that of his pen, scratching against paper. A humorless laugh caught in her chest, but she managed to squelch it.

As she walked back to the elevators, Denise told herself that it was a good thing that he had forgotten about her. At least, she wasn't in trouble for skipping out on work. She should be happy at the way things had turned out.

Seven

It was as if she were a comic book superhero.

Like Clark Kent, Denise was leading a double life. By day, she was a mild-mannered, stuck-in-a-rut accountant. She said the right things, wore the right clothes and danced attendance on her father. In short, she did everything she was expected to do.

By night though, she had become someone quite different.

Someone she was enjoying.

Denise glanced at her reflection and smiled in amazement. If someone had told her three weeks ago that she would be wearing black leather pants, black boots and a red sweatshirt with the Harley-Davidson logo on it, she would have laughed at them.

She shoved two silver clips in her hair at either

side of her head, then grimaced slightly. No matter how much fun her secret identity had become, she didn't think she would ever get used to flat "helmet" hair.

But that was a small price to pay for discovering this new Denise Torrance.

"And," she told herself, "Mike was right about the leather pants being warmer." When she wore jeans on their nightly rides, the icy sea air seemed to cut right through the denim.

She sat down on the edge of her quilt-covered bed and reached for her boots. As she yanked them on and stomped into them, she wondered where Mike was taking her tonight.

Over the last week or so, the two of them had hopped onto his motorcycle every night to ride off in search of another adventure. Besides a few return visits to O'Doul's, there had been quiet dinners in tiny, out-of-the-way restaurants, and even once, a trip to Tijuana.

At that thought, she looked up at her mirror again. Tucked into the frame was a photo of she and Mike, wearing sombreros, sitting astride two stuffed donkeys.

Silly, but she had never had so much fun.

A curl of excitement spiraled in her stomach. He would be here any minute, she knew. Denise felt as giddy as a high school kid on prom night. But then, she admitted silently, she had felt that way almost every night since meeting him. She deliberately ignored a niggling thread of worry. They hadn't done anything foolish again. There had been no more wild, out-of-control lovemaking sessions.

Instead, they spent time together. Talked. Laughed. And the desire between them grew hotter, stronger.

Yet in its own way, that was just as dangerous. She stared at that photo again, her gaze locking onto Mike's image. Over the past few days, the feelings she had for him had changed, gone beyond that initial attraction.

Denise drew one long, shaky breath and jumped to her feet. Her head swam and the room spun around her in dizzying circles. Closing her eyes, she carefully sat back down and waited for the odd sensations to pass.

Her mind raced with more questions than she had answers. The period she had expected to arrive that morning hadn't. But it was too early to start worrying, wasn't it?

In seconds, she was fine again. When the doorbell rang, she stood up slowly. Once she was sure she wouldn't fall over, she went to answer it.

He cut the engine, set the kickstand into place then climbed off the bike and stood waiting on the driveway. Denise pulled her helmet off, looked at him, then shifted her gaze to the small house just a few feet away.

One light shone from behind the curtains at the front window, spilling onto a tiny lawn banked by a riot of flowers, their colors muted now by summer moonlight.

"Who lives here?" she asked, wondering if they were visiting some of his friends.

"I do."

Denise swiveled her head to look up at him from her perch on the bike. Interesting. Somehow she hadn't imagined him living in a tidy Cape Cod. He seemed more the efficiency apartment type. No ties, no sentiment. Beige walls and communal hot tubs.

Curious, she let her gaze sweep across the small, well-kept yard to the three-foot-tall picket fence surrounding the property. Unlike most neighborhoods in beach cities, the old houses on this street weren't jammed too close together. At least fifty years old, they had been built before land in California became so valuable that contractors now shoved twenty houses onto lots meant for fifteen.

This house had character. A personality.

"I like it," she said.

"Thanks." Mike's defensive posture relaxed. It was almost as if he had been prepared for her to hate the place. He glanced at the house and said, "It used to belong to my grandparents. They moved in right after their wedding."

"No honeymoon?" she teased

Mike winked at her. "Grandpa Ryan always claimed that this was the best honeymoon cottage in the world."

A wistful pang erupted in her chest as she turned back to look at the little house again. In her mind's eye, she saw that long-ago young couple, coming to this house to start their life together. In a flash, she saw the years pass, children grow, grandchildren born and still that once young couple were together. Loving each other.

How nice it must have been she thought, to grow up seeing that kind of love.

Her own memories were less pleasant.

"Are they still—" She stopped, unsure of how best to ask that particular question. Yet she wanted to know. She somehow *needed* to know that his grandparents' love continued.

"Alive?" he finished for her. "Yeah."

Denise smiled, relieved.

"They moved to Phoenix a few years ago," Mike explained. "Grandpa said the ocean damp was bothering Gran, but I think he just wanted to live right on top of a golf course."

Ridiculous, she knew, to be so pleased that two people she didn't even know were still healthy and together. Her gaze slid across the wooden shutters at the windows, the shake roof and the flowering vines creeping along a trellis attached to a side wall of the house.

"I know you and Patrick are twins," she said softly as she realized that Mike had told her almost nothing about his family. "Are there any other Ryans I should know about?"

He helped her off the bike, flicked up the kickstand again and pushed the motorcycle down the short drive to the garage beyond the house. "Besides Patrick and me, there's Sean and Dennis. Sean's the oldest, then Dennis."

Denise followed him, listening. "Didn't any of them want this house?"

"Get one of the doors for me?" he asked and waited while she opened one side of the double doors to the too-small-for-a-car garage. "Sean's stationed in South Carolina. Dennis has a houseboat moored south of here and you couldn't blast Patrick out of his apartment," Mike said with a laugh.

"He's gone now," she reminded him.

"Only on vacation."

She leaned against the garage wall and watched him as he set the kickstand again and stepped away from the bike. "You said Sean is stationed up north?"

"Yeah." Mike reached up, yanked the cord on a bare lightbulb, then turned to look at her in the dim glow. He shoved both hands into the back pockets of his jeans. "Career marine."

His features tightened and a muscle in his jaw twitched. He suddenly looked more like he had that first night in Patrick's office than he had in more than a week. Why? "You have something against the marines?" she asked.

"Not for Sean, I guess. He likes it. I didn't."

"You were in the service?"

"Eight years. Got out a few years back."

His answers were getting shorter. Sharper. Maybe she should have left it alone and backed away from what was apparently a tender subject. But she didn't.

"Why did you leave?"

He dragged a deep breath into his lungs and even in the indistinct light of that low wattage bulb, Denise saw the strain in his features. "Let's just say I saw enough of the desert to last me a lifetime."

Desert?

A cold chill ran down the length of her spine and she shivered. A marine in the desert. His grim expression. He had to have been involved in the Gulf War. She looked at him, trying to see behind the shutters he had erected over his eyes. Trying to see what that experience had done to him. But she couldn't. He was much too good at hiding his feelings behind a hard-as-nails mask.

At the same time, she realized that but for good fortune, he might have died in that desert war and she would never have met him. Never have known what it felt like to be held by him. Never have gotten to know the woman she had become since meeting him.

She couldn't imagine not knowing Mike. Her gaze settled on his features and she realized just how much he had come to mean to her. How much she looked forward to seeing him. Talking to him. How much she felt for him, despite her best intentions. What if they had never met? she wondered.

Another, deeper chill touched her and this time, he reacted when she shivered. He yanked the light cord again, plunging the tiny garage into darkness. "Come on," he said tightly. "You're cold."

She had caused this tension in him, by unintentionally stirring up old memories and now she wanted to dispel it. Denise wanted the real Mike back. The man she knew and cared for. As he came close, she said abruptly, "It must have been fun. Growing up with three brothers, I mean."

He walked to her side and as his features became

clearer in the darkness, she saw a wry smile lifting one corner of his mouth. Apparently, he was relieved with the change of subject.

"Oh, yeah." He set one hand on the plank wall beside her head and leaned in close. "It was a blast. Yelling, fighting. Every day was Disneyland."

"You enjoyed it," she guessed.

"Every minute." He lifted his left hand to stroke her cheek. "What about you? Brothers? Sisters?"

Her breath caught at his touch. "No. None."

"Must have been lonely."

"And quiet." Maybe she wouldn't have been so lonely if she and her father hadn't been so far apart. Maybe… She cut short that line of thinking. It did no good to keep raking over the past. Denise sucked in a gulp of air and tried to keep the conversation moving.

The tiny garage suddenly seemed claustrophobic and it had everything to do with the fact that Mike was standing way too close to allow coherent thought.

"What about your parents?" she asked.

He chuckled, as if he knew exactly what she was thinking, before taking a step back from her. Then, leading the way out of the garage he said over his shoulder, "Both retired."

"From what?" she asked as he shut the door behind them and headed for the back porch of the house.

"Ever hear of Wave Cutters?"

"Of course. It's one of the biggest surfboard companies in southern California."

"That's the one." He unlocked the back door, opened it and ushered Denise in ahead of him.

She blinked at the brightness when he flicked the kitchen light on. A scrubbed pine pedestal table sat in the center of the big, square room and in the middle of the table was a huge, wicker picnic basket. As Mike moved to the refrigerator, she said, "Wave Cutters makes surfboards, wet suits, beach wear...just about everything."

"That's them."

"Them who?" she asked as he pulled a bottle of wine and a plate of sandwiches from the fridge and set them on the table.

"My parents. *They're* Wave Cutters." He stopped, shrugged. "Well, they were. Now, it's Dennis's headache."

"Headache?" Denise pulled one of the captain's chairs out and plopped down onto it. "You didn't want to be a part of your family's business?"

"Nope." He looked over the edge of the door and winked at her. "Well, all four of us are actually on the board, but Dennis is in charge. The rest of us just collect dividends."

"Why?" Wasn't he proud of what his parents had accomplished? Wave Cutters was one of the fastest growing companies in the country. "How could you not want to be a part of it? Your parents must have been furious."

"Furious?" Mike laughed out loud at that one. "My dad believes in doing what you want to do. *His* dad had wanted him to go into business with him—TV repair. Said that surfing and being a beach bum would never support a family.'' He shook his head. ''Tell my dad 'No' and it's like issuing a direct challenge.''

Like father like son, she thought.

''Anyway, when Wave Cutters took off, Grandpa sold his business and went to work for his son.'' Mike stood up, shut the fridge and leaned back against the door, smiling at her. ''Together, they built it up so well, they both retired to do what they love best.''

''Golfing.''

''For Grandpa,'' Mike agreed. ''My folks, though, bought a place in Hawaii.'' His black eyebrows wiggled and his eyes sparkled in amusement. ''They're looking for the perfect wave.''

Denise shook her head. Her own father seldom left his office. And Mike's father walked out on a hugely successful company to be a full-time surfer? She could just imagine what Richard Torrance would think of that.

''What's the matter?'' Mike walked to her side and squatted down beside the chair. ''Disappointed to find out that I've got money? That I'm not the dangerous desperado you thought I was?''

She looked into his green eyes and saw that he was actually worried about what she was thinking. Not dangerous? she thought. One look into his eyes and her toes curled and sparks skittered down her backbone. She drew a series of shallow breaths and forced her heart into a regular beat again. ''Oh, you're dangerous all right, Ryan.''

He grinned at her and her pulse jumped into jackhammer time again. "Good," he said. "I prefer dangerous to successful businessman."

Denise didn't understand that at all, but didn't bother to say so. At the moment, she was less interested in what he did for a living than in what he did to her. She stood up when he pulled her from the chair. Her vision blurred slightly at the quick movement and she leaned her forehead against his chest briefly.

"Hey," he asked, "are you all right?"

She pulled in a long breath, drawing the scent of Old Spice deep into her lungs. As the dizziness passed, she nodded. "Fine. I just got up too fast."

Mike looked at her warily. "You're sure that's all it is?"

Not entirely, Denise thought with a pang, but said only, "I'm sure."

He nodded abruptly. "In that case, let's get going."

"To where?" she asked.

Mike picked up the now full basket and gave her a slow smile. "A picnic."

High, craggy cliff walls surrounded him on three sides. Mike glanced skyward and sighed heavily. Maybe this hadn't been such a good idea, he told himself. Moonlight, an empty beach, a sheltered cove and Denise. Through hooded eyes, he watched her, standing only inches from the incoming tide.

Soft light from the full moon fell on her in iridescent patterns of shimmering silver. She lifted her wineglass to take a long drink and his gaze locked on the elegant column of her throat. Ocean air lifted her hair and teased the curls into a tangled mess that only served to make her more beautiful. The leather pants he'd given her for riding hugged her legs with a lover's grasp.

His hands itched to touch her. His body ached with a pain that had tormented him for the past ten days. She never left his mind. And that fact terrified him almost as much as the thought of never seeing her again.

But this couldn't go on and he knew it. Once they found out if she was pregnant or not, a decision would have to be made. If she *was* pregnant... Instantly, his mind conjured an image of her lithe body rounded with the swell of his child. He groaned quietly as he realized she would be even more beautiful to him pregnant than she was now. He rubbed one hand over his eyes and told himself not to think about that yet. There was a good possibility that she *wasn't* going to have a baby. And if not, she would probably want him out of her life. Though that was most likely for the best, it bothered him to realize just how much he had come to count on seeing her every day.

To know how much she meant to him.

"Hey!"

He let go of his thoughts and looked at her.

"Are you going to hog all that wine to yourself?" She held out her empty wineglass toward him.

"You've had enough," he said, and wondered how anyone could get tipsy on one glass of white wine.

"Half a glass more," she called back over the roar of the ocean.

He shook his head, got up and walked to her side. Taking her glass, he filled it a quarter of the way and handed it back to her.

She nodded a thank you then reached up to push her windblown hair out of her face. So different from the woman who had tried to attack him with pepper spray. She looked relaxed. Happy.

And way too tempting.

"It's beautiful out here, Mike." She grinned at him. "I've never been to a picnic on the beach."

"In a couple of more weeks, this place will be so crowded, you wouldn't find a spot to throw a blanket down."

"I like it like this," she told him and leaned closer. "Empty. Private."

He told himself that she had had too many. That there were rules about things like this. You just didn't take advantage of a woman when her defenses were down. No matter how tantalizing the invitation.

"I know what you're thinking," she said and pressed herself against him. "You think I'm drunk."

"A little."

"Not even a little," Denise said and met his gaze squarely, soberly. The wind brushed a lock of hair across her eyes again and she reached up to push it out of the way.

He set his hands at her waist to steady her as she leaned her slight weight into him. Every spot where her body met his was suddenly alive. His fingers tightened on her narrow waist. He looked down into her eyes and called himself a fool.

Only a couple of hours ago, his memories of desert warfare had been all too close to the surface. For one brief moment there in the garage, he had been able to feel the blazing heat of the sun. The scent of fear and sweat had surrounded him.

And with those memories had come another. The memory of a promise he had made to himself. To steer clear of love. To avoid giving anyone the power to hurt him as his friends and their families had been hurt.

Yet here he was, coming dangerously close to caring for a woman who even now might be carrying his child.

"Denise," he said abruptly, "when will we know about—"

She reached up and laid her fingertips over his mouth, effectively silencing him. "I'll buy a test tomorrow."

Tomorrow. A thousand differing emotions battled within him for dominance. He had never planned on being a father. Had figured on leaving all of that to his brothers. But, now that he was actually faced with the prospect of a child, it was different. Surprising as it was to admit, he had caught himself almost hoping there *would* be a baby. A girl maybe, with Denise's blue eyes and blond hair.

Something inside him shifted painfully. Was it the child he wanted…or was it *her* child that had suddenly become so important?

"We'll know for sure tomorrow," she said, "one way or the other."

He nodded.

"But tonight, Mike," she continued and her soft voice was almost lost in the pulsing rush of the ocean, "let's forget about everything but us. I want one more night with you before we know. Before things change forever."

Mike bit back a groan as an invisible hand tightened around his heart and squeezed. Her quiet words tore at him, leaving his insides open and unguarded.

"Kiss me, Mike."

A deep, throbbing ache settled low in his gut and his hands fisted at his sides to keep from reaching for her. He looked down into her face, brushed by moonglow, and silently admitted that he had also been hoping this would happen. He had counted on the moon and the stars and the seductive scent and sound of the ocean to urge her into his arms.

Why bother pretending now that he wasn't interested?

Mike groaned again as he grabbed her and pulled her into the circle of his arms. He lowered his mouth to hers like a dying man seeking salvation and dismissed the last of his guilt in the rush of need swamping him. No point in denying the truth to himself. He had to have her.

Eight

She dropped the glass to the sand and when he tore his mouth from hers to lavish long, slow, wet kisses along her throat, her moan of pleasure heightened his every sense.

Mike couldn't wait any longer. He had already lived through the longest ten days of his life. Quickly, he scooped her up into his arms and practically ran back to their blanket. Setting her on her feet again, he yanked her sweatshirt off. As she unhooked her bra, he tore off his own shirt and threw it to the sand.

He grabbed her again, pulling her flush against him. He wanted to feel all of her. Touch all of her. The cold air blowing in off the water couldn't dampen the heat devouring them. Moonlight made her skin gleam like fine porcelain and he ran his hands up and down her back, relishing the smoothness of her skin. Denise's hands clutched at his shoulders and every one of her fingertips acted as a brand, searing him with tiny darts of fire that reached down into a soul too long untouched.

Anxious fingers fumbled with snaps and zippers. Her breath came in short, sharp pants, brushing his skin with warmth. Flames erupted inside him. His heart pounded fiercely and breathing became secondary. All he wanted, all he *needed* was her. Her touch. Her kiss. The silky grip of her body on his. He bent his head to take one of her nipples into his mouth. She arched against him, her fingernails digging into his shoulders.

''Mike,'' she whispered on a moan. He heard his own torment and need echoed in her strained voice.

Deliberately, he ran the edges of his teeth over her rigid nipple. Denise gasped and moved one hand to the back of his head, holding him in place. She needn't have worried that he would stop. If it had meant his life, he couldn't have left her. Drawing on that sensitive bud, he suckled her, tugging on her flesh with a steadily increasing pressure that pushed her forward, toward the edge of a precipice they had both dangled from for days.

As he gave first one breast, then the other, his devoted attention, his hands smoothed underwear and those black leather pants down her legs. He lowered his head farther, trailing kisses along her rib cage, across her abdomen and finally, on the triangle of curls guarding her secrets.

Denise swayed unsteadily on her feet and he

tightened his hold on her. With him bracing her, she stepped out of her clothes and stood before him, wearing only the glimmer of moonlight.

"You're so beautiful," he murmured as his fingers traveled up her inner thighs. "More beautiful than I remembered."

Her breath caught and she grabbed at his shoulders again for balance. "Mike," she whispered, "don't make me wait. Make love to me again."

"I will, honey," he promised and gently nudged her thighs farther apart. "Nothing can keep us apart tonight." Holding on to her hips, Mike slowly leaned close and dragged a line of kisses along her belly. Her legs trembled. His grip on her hips tightened and he dipped his head to taste the heart of her.

"Mike!" she gasped his name and dug her fingernails deeper into his shoulder muscles.

Tremors rippled through her, leaving him shaken. He ran the tip of his tongue across one small, hard bud and felt her body quiver in response. Damp heat welcomed him and Mike gave himself over to the pleasure of loving her. Each gasp of delight that shot from her throat only fed the raging desire burning inside him.

"It feels so...good," she managed to say softly, brokenly.

Her legs stiffened, her hips rocked against his mouth as she tried to open herself even further to him.

He smoothed his tongue across that so tender spot and as he did, his right hand slipped to the valley between her thighs. His lips and tongue stroked her velvety softness and Mike gently dipped two fingers into the tight, hot sheath of her body.

She tensed, every muscle suddenly going rigid.

He redoubled his attentions. His fingers slid in and out of her damp heat and his mouth tantalized her.

She widened her stance, welcoming him, silently demanding the release that he knew was rushing toward her. A soft, broken cry issued from her throat when the first ripples of satisfaction shuddered through her. She held the back of his head to her and Mike groaned along with her as if her release were his own.

Staggering and limp, Denise leaned against him and he eased her gently down onto the blanket. She gave him a wan smile.

"Mike, I never knew that I could feel something like that. So..." Her eyes slid shut briefly and she paused to take a long, shuddering breath. When she opened her eyes again, she reached for him, lifting still trembling arms.

Quickly, unwilling to wait another moment to be joined with her, he shucked his boots and jeans. He paused only long enough to fumble through his wallet, before tossing it atop his clothes. Then he turned back to her, already tearing open a small foil packet.

She looked up at him and smiled. Lazily, she asked, "Isn't that like locking the barn door after the horse is out and running?"

Mike slid the sheath on, then moved to kneel between legs she parted in invitation. Grinning down at her, he said, "This time lady, we do things *right*."

"My hero."

"Damn straight."

Denise lifted her hips as he entered her. Though the flush of release still warmed her, she was immediately roused again. As his strong, hard body moved in and out of hers, she felt another driving need building inside.

Tension streaked through her body. She held her breath, sure that this time, the climax would kill her. She held him tighter, anchoring herself to his strength. Fireworks exploded within her. Her hips moved in time with his. Hands caressed. Lips met in hungry kisses that left them gasping for air. One last thrust and her body convulsed around his. He called her name as he fell into her arms and Denise used the last of her energy to catch him and hold him tightly.

The solid, heavy weight of him pressed down on her and beneath the blanket they lay on, she felt the hills and valleys of sand digging into her back. Still, she didn't want to move. She wanted time to stop. She wanted this moment to last forever.

Tomorrow, they would know if they had created a baby and everything between them would change. A sheen of tears pricked at her eyes and Denise blinked them back as she held Mike even tighter.

They had no future. From the beginning, she had known that Mike Ryan was the wrong man for her. They were too different. They had nothing in common. Except perhaps, she thought, a child.

But she knew better than anyone that a child wasn't enough to keep two people happy. Her own parents had failed miserably and she refused to re-live their mistakes.

Not even for Mike.

God help her, she loved him. She didn't know how it had happened, or even when and it didn't really matter. All that mattered was that she loved a man she couldn't have. Her eyes slid closed as she wondered how she would ever get through the rest of her life without him.

Her deep, even breathing told him she was asleep. Mike tightened his arms around her, drawing her even closer against his side. Her breath puffed on his naked chest, she mumbled something incoherent and slid one of her hands across his abdomen to rest on his hip.

Mike glanced at the window on the far wall and saw the first stirrings of dawn beginning to lighten the sky. Soon, it would be morning. Soon, he would find out if he was about to become a father or not.

His eyes squeezed shut briefly. Then he opened them again to stare up at the ceiling. How the hell could she sleep? he wondered. In just a few short hours now, their lives might be changed forever.

He lifted one hand to smooth across her hair, lov-ing the feel of the soft silky curls against his palm. She muttered again and shifted at his side. Mike took a long, deep breath and smiled into the dark-ness. Strange how right it felt, her body aligned with his, lying together in the big bed his grandparents had founded a family in.

"Mike?" she whispered and he bent his head to look into her face. Asleep, he told himself. Asleep and talking. He wondered if she knew about this little habit of hers.

Easing his head back down onto the pillows, he stroked her back gently and said quietly, "Shh, Denise. It's all right."

"Mmm..." She sighed and cuddled in closer.

His body immediately hardened. Desire and a deep-seated need to protect swelled up within him, fighting for precedence. Protection won.

"Sleep, baby," he crooned gently as he continued to stroke her skin reassuringly.

"I love you, Mike," Denise mumbled.

He held his breath.

She muttered something more, but he didn't quite catch it. It didn't matter, though. He had heard enough.

Snatches of emotions raced through him. Fear, wonder, pleasure. Love. She loved him.

In her sleep, he thought. Wide awake, he doubted very much that she would have said those three words. But did that make a difference? No. And how did *he* feel? Was this strange, unsettled feeling in the pit of his stomach love? And if it was, what should he do about it? He wasn't husband material, was he? As for being a father... God, he pitied the kid who was stuck with *him* for a parent.

A kid deserved someone who was good at all of the things parents were supposed to be good at.

Right? What did he know abut PTAs and bingo nights and booster clubs? Wasn't that stuff important?

But his own childhood had been a good one, he told himself, and as far as he could remember, his old man had never gone to a single parent-teacher conference. Maybe, he thought, it was enough just to love your kid.

Wrapping both arms around Denise, he rested his chin on the top of her head. He didn't have any answers and Lord knew, the thought of parenthood still scared the hell out of him. But despite all of that, he silently promised the woman in his arms that everything would be all right.

"How much longer?" Mike asked again.

Denise checked the kitchen timer sitting on the bathroom sink. "About another minute."

"Are you sure you set that thing for three minutes?"

"Yes, I'm sure." She couldn't really blame him for growling. Three minutes had never felt so long to her, either. And Mike's tiny bathroom seemed to be shrinking. The two of them had been standing there, just a foot apart for two full minutes, waiting for an answer to the question that had been in the backs of their minds for ten days.

She glanced at him briefly, but couldn't bear to look into those shuttered eyes of his. Whatever he was thinking, he was keeping to himself.

Unable to stand still a moment longer, she snatched up the pregnancy kit's instruction sheet, stuffed it into the empty box then tossed it into the trash. Trying to keep busy, she also tried not to stare at the test stick. She looked at Mike again, standing in the open doorway to his house's one and only bathroom. She saw him watching that stick as if expecting it to blow up any second.

She wished she was home. In her own house. Denise rubbed her upper arms nervously. Somehow, this whole test thing would have been easier to handle if she had been in familiar surroundings. Alone.

Blast it, she had planned to buy a kit herself, take the darn test in private and then inform Mike of the results. It would have given her time to adjust to whatever those results were. But she was beginning to understand that *nothing* worked out as planned. When they had finally left the beach the night before, they were both too tired to take a step beyond his house.

She had fallen asleep in Mike's arms and awakened to find him already up and gone. He returned armed with a box of donuts and an early pregnancy test kit. Now all that was left to do was wait.

Denise studied his expression covertly. Tense, grim, he was no doubt silently muttering every prayer he had ever known in the hopes of keeping that stick from turning pink.

The only real question here was, why wasn't she doing the same thing?

A shrill bell rang out suddenly and Denise jumped. Mike took one long step into the room and shut off the timer. Looking at her, he asked unnecessarily, "One pink stripe, negative, two stripes positive, right?"

She nodded, knowing as well as he did that neither of them was likely to forget how to read the stick. Too much was riding on the answers. She took a deep breath and swallowed hard past an unexpected lump of emotion clogging her throat.

"You want to look," Mike prompted, "or do you want me to?"

"Go ahead." She closed her eyes and waited. It didn't matter who looked, she told herself. The answer would be the same. And her hope for privacy had already been shattered.

A long moment passed in silence, then Mike said flatly, "That's it then."

"What?" she asked, even though she knew what he meant.

"Congratulations, Ms. Torrance," he said. "It's a baby."

Did the room spin or was it just her mind racing, whirling with a sudden overload?

"Ohmigod," she said as air rushed from her lungs. "Let me see it."

"I know pink when I see it," his voice rumbled into the small room. "And even I can count to two."

Still, she held her hand out for the slender white wand. She needed to see it herself. She needed to look down at the bright pink stripes that had just thrown her life a serious curve. He slapped it into her palm. She stared down at the test square and then the control square. Each of them held a distinct pink line.

Pregnant.

"I need to sit down," she muttered and turned toward the door, still clutching that stick.

She walked down the short hall to the living room and practically fell onto the old, overstuffed sofa. She wasn't surprised. Stunned maybe, but not surprised. Somehow it only made sense that the one time she stepped out of her usual world...the one time she had acted before thinking...would end in a baby.

Fathered by the one man she should never have loved.

"You okay?" he asked.

Denise looked up at him, standing in front of the sofa, arms crossed over his chest. My, he looked delighted.

"Yes. I think so," she said, leaning back into the cushions. She reached up and rubbed her forehead, hoping to ease the headache that had just erupted behind her eyes. "A little...confused at the moment, but okay."

"Well," he countered, "I'm not."

Her eyebrows lifted. Not real surprising, she thought. He had made his feelings more than clear on the night this child had been conceived. It might have been nice if he didn't look as though he were about to face a firing squad. On the other hand, at least she knew exactly where he stood. Which should make living without him a bit easier to deal with.

After all, what kind of future could she have had

anyway with a man who so clearly had no desire to be a father?

She didn't want to examine too closely the wrench of disappointment that tugged at her. She had no right to be let down or hurt at his reaction. Logically, she knew that. Unfortunately, logic didn't have a lot to do with what she was feeing at the time.

The thing to do, she told herself, was to go home. Get back to her own place where she could sit and think, out from under Mike Ryan's glare.

"Thanks for being honest," she said stiffly and started to get up.

"You didn't let me finish," Mike said sharply.

"Oh, I think you were fairly clear."

"Dammit, will you listen for a minute?"

"Why should I? Just by looking at you I can tell what you want to say." Her voice sounded more strained than she would have wanted ordinarily. But under the circumstances, she felt as though she was doing pretty well.

"Is that right?" he said, his own voice harsh and scratchy.

"It's perfectly obvious, Mike. You're upset about our...*news*. Well, that's understandable." She tried to get up, but he laid one hand on her shoulder, holding her down gently. She stared at that hand until he pulled it away. "But it should be just as understandable to you that I need to be alone for a while. To think."

"Thinking can wait another minute or two, all right?"

One minute. All right, she would give him one minute to tell her that he wasn't going to be trapped into being a father. Then she would let him know that she had no intention of springing that trap, either. Easing back into the sofa cushions, she drew her knees close to her chest and wrapped her arms around her legs. "Fine. I'll listen."

He reached up and used both hands to smooth his hair back from his face. When he was finished, he tucked his palms into the back pockets of his jeans. Staring down at her, the familiar shutters over his eyes, he said, "I didn't mean that I'm not okay. I meant, I'm not confused."

Now, *she* was more confused than ever.

"We've got some decisions to make, Denise."

"I'm not ready to make any decisions yet, Mike." This life-altering news was only about two minutes old. She needed a tad more time to be able to think rationally.

"It's not like you haven't known this moment might be coming."

"I knew the chance was there," she countered, "but I didn't really think it would happen." Her head dropped back to rest on the top edge of the sofa. On a groan, she added, "It was just the one time."

A half smile crossed his features briefly. "I wonder how many couples have used that particular phrase over the last thousand years?"

She didn't know and she didn't care. Denise had all she could do at the moment to concentrate on her. On this baby and what it meant in her life. Good God. *Her?* A *mother?*

Her gaze flicked to Mike. In his usual biker outfit, he didn't look like anyone's ideal of a father. Oh Lord, father. *Her* father. How would she tell her father this?

What would he say when...*if* he met Mike?

The headache became a driving, pounding force that drummed inside her head in time with her heartbeat. Every aching pulse screeched at her.

Suddenly too tightly wound to sit still, she jumped up from the couch. A wave of dizziness crashed down on her and she wobbled a bit before falling backward onto the sofa.

Instantly, Mike was there, kneeling in front of her. "Are you all right?"

"I'm fine. Just a little dizzy." And how long would this be happening to her? Lord, her entire world was sliding out of control and she was helpless to stop it.

"Again?" Mike demanded. "Is that normal?"

Patience suddenly gone, she glared directly into his green eyes and snapped, "How would I know? I've never been pregnant before." Her stomach pitched violently. Funny how just saying the word out loud made it so *real.* And so terrifying. "Oh, God," she whispered and clamped one hand over her mouth as she pushed past him and raced back to the bathroom.

Mike held her head and she was too miserable to care that he was seeing her in such a disgusting state. When her stomach was finally empty, he soaked a cloth in cold water, wrung it out and gently wiped her face. Then he lifted her from the floor and carried her to his bedroom. Laying her down on the mattress, he straightened up and started pacing.

Wrapped in her own misery, Denise didn't even notice when he came to a sudden stop.

"This pregnancy changes things," he said.

She opened one eye to look at him. "What things?" she muttered. "Besides the obvious, I mean?"

"Things between us."

There it was. It hadn't taken him long to recover fully enough to let her know he wanted their friendship to end. Well, she had known the moment she had agreed to go out with him that their time together would be short.

She was hardly the sort of woman he usually spent time with. And as for her, a man in black was so far removed from the usual ambitious, driven business-suit types she normally dated, it would have been laughable. If it all wasn't so damn sad.

Why had she fallen in love with him? Why hadn't she stopped this relationship before it started? She knew what could happen if a woman fell in love with the wrong man. Her own mother had been miserable.

The woman had loved Richard Torrance to distraction. And Richard had had time only for his business. He was a man who should never have married.

A man like Mike.

Oh, not that the two men were really alike in any way except one. Neither of them were interested in marriage. Somehow her mother had convinced Richard to take a chance. Denise wasn't going to make the same mistake.

"Don't worry about it, Mike," she said and pushed herself up onto one elbow. Pausing, she waited a moment to see if her stomach was going to rebel. When she was sure she was safe, she went on, forcing herself to look at him calmly. "I don't expect anything from you. I'll take care of—everything myself."

"Oh, thanks so much." Sarcasm dripped from every word.

She blinked. He sounded angry.

Furious, Mike simply stared at her. Did she really think so little of him? Did she just assume that he would do a quick-fade out the minute they found out she was pregnant? With *his* baby?

Of course she did. What else could she think? He had told her himself that he wasn't interested in love and marriage. He shoved one hand through his hair, then viciously rubbed the back of his neck. Looking at her again, he stared into wide blue eyes filled with confusion, and he *knew* what had to be done.

"There's no reason for you to take care of anything all by yourself."

"Mike..."

"Marry me."

"*What?*" She sat bolt upright on the bed.

He inhaled sharply, cleared his throat and forced the words out again. Barely. "Marry me, Denise."

"You're out of your mind."

"No, I'm not. I'm trying to find a way out of this for both—all *three* of us," he corrected himself.

"That's not a way out Mike," she said, with a slow shake of her head. "That's the way in. To deeper trouble."

"No, it's not." Talking fast now, he sat down on the end of the mattress and held her gaze. "It could work. We get along well. Neither one of us is a kid, we'd be able to work together. And you have to admit that two parents are better than one."

"Not if they don't want to be together."

"Fine, I admit that I never thought I'd get married."

Two blond eyebrows lifted.

"But I didn't have a reason before."

"You don't *now,* either."

"There's the baby."

"Mike, this is the nineties. There are all sorts of solutions to this kind of problem besides the one you're suggesting."

"Problem?" he repeated. "This isn't a problem, Denise. It's a baby. *My* baby."

She looked at him for a long moment, then scooted to the edge of the bed and stood up. "It's *my* baby too, Ryan. And I'm not going to be pushed into doing something I think is wrong just because you've decided to play storybook hero."

"What?"

"This knight in shining armor thing." Color flushed her pale cheeks. "I don't need to be rescued, Mike. I'm a big girl and I can take care of myself."

She turned quickly and started for the hall. He

caught her in two steps. Grabbing her arm, he turned her around to look at him. "You're not going to shut me out of this, Denise. It's my child and I deserve a say in what happens to him."

"We didn't even *know* about her until fifteen minutes ago," she said quietly, but firmly. "I think she deserves better than her parents making a decision without even bothering to think about it."

"Now isn't the time to think," he snapped. "It's a time to *feel.* Sometimes you have to go with your gut, Denise. You can't think everything to death."

"*Feelings* are exactly what brought us to this point, Mike. If we had stopped to think two weeks ago, neither of us would be standing here having this conversation."

She was right. He didn't like it, but she was right. Oh, not about two weeks ago. Nothing could make him regret that night with her. Not even this surprise pregnancy. But she did deserve a little more time to come to the conclusion that his was the only possible solution.

So maybe he wouldn't have proposed if there hadn't been a baby. But there *is* a baby. And that tiny life meant the rules had just changed on the game they had been playing. She could take all the time she wanted, but Mike wasn't going anywhere.

"All right," he said and released her. The battle gleam in her eyes faded a bit as she took a step back. "Take some time. Do some thinking. So will I."

"Good."

"I'll come by your place tonight and we'll talk again."

"Tonight?"

"Yeah. We can talk this whole thing out then."

She stepped into the hall, keeping her gaze locked with his. "Not tonight. I need a few days to myself, Mike. I'll call you, okay?"

"You're not planning on doing something and telling me about it later, are you?" he muttered thickly.

Realization dawned in her eyes and she shook her head. "No. No, I promise I won't do anything until I've told you what my decision is."

"Your decision?"

"It's your baby too, Mike, but it's inside *me*. The final decision will be mine."

Nine

Five days later, she was no closer to a decision. True to his word, Mike had kept his distance. But now, Denise couldn't help wondering if he was staying away because she had asked him to—or because he had realized that his marriage proposal was a mistake.

She was still rational enough to know that she wasn't being fair. But emotional enough not to care.

And Lord, how she missed him.

"Denise?" Richard Torrance walked into his daughter's office, a sheaf of papers clenched tightly in one hand.

"Hmmm?" She turned her back on the view of the ocean to face the man's slowly purpling features. "Father, what's wrong?"

"Wrong?" he echoed. "Oh nothing, except that I almost had heart failure a moment ago."

"What are you talking about?"

"These figures, Denise," he said and waved the papers in his fist. "On the Steenberg account? According to your calculations, their company lost several hundred thousand dollars last month."

"I don't under—"

"You transposed the numbers, Denise. If I hadn't caught your error, Mr. Steenberg probably *would* have had a heart attack!"

"I'm sorry," she said and sat back in her chair. Propping her elbows on the polished wooden arms, she briefly cupped her face in her hands. There went her last safety net. She couldn't even count on numbers anymore.

"You've been sorry for nearly a week." He dropped the papers onto her desk, flattened his palms on the maroon leather blotter and demanded, "Where has your mind gone, girl?"

She lifted her head to stare at him. "I'm not a girl, father."

"You're certainly behaving like one," he countered hotly. "Canceling appointments, coming in late, leaving early. If you weren't my own flesh and blood, I would have fired you days ago."

She jumped to her feet, waited for the now familiar touch of dizziness to pass, then met her father's glare with one of her own. If he had been more interested in his daughter's welfare rather than his employee's performance, he would know what the problem was. She would have been able to talk to him. Ask his advice.

Instead, they were further apart than ever, whether he knew it or not. And today, she was too tired to put up with it. Too exhausted to worry about saying just the right thing, she said flatly, "Fine. Fire me."

Richard jerked his head back, clearly as surprised as he would have been to have a lamp jump off the desk and bite him.

Reaching down into her bottom desk drawer, Denise pulled her huge purse out and slung the strap over her shoulder. Digging into the bag, she pulled out her bottle of antacids and shook two of them into the center of her palm. Before she popped them into her mouth though, she stopped and wondered if antacids were safe for the baby. She didn't know. Lately, she felt as though she didn't know *anything*. Carefully, she scooped the tablets back into the bottle, then dropped the container into her purse. Better to be safe than sorry.

"What do you mean, fire you?" Richard asked, his tone demanding an answer. "What has gotten into you?"

Briefly, she considered blurting out, "A baby." But thought better of it. One thing she didn't need at the moment was her father's opinion on her impending motherhood.

Instead, she said, "I mean, father, if you're that unhappy with my work, fire me as you would any other employee. I won't have trouble finding a job. Any accounting firm in this town would be *glad* to hire me."

"I didn't say—"

"Yes, you did, Father. And you know what? I don't care." As she said the words, she realized the truth in them and felt her tension level drop just a little. Inhaling sharply, she came out from behind her desk and marched past him, toward the door. Before she left though, she looked over her shoulder at him. "I'll probably be late again tomorrow. I haven't been feeling well."

He opened his mouth to speak, but she cut him off cleanly.

"If I'm not working here any longer, leave word with my secretary. I'll pack up my things and be out by tomorrow afternoon." She turned on her heel and stormed past the secretaries in the main room, each of them staring at her as if she had sprouted another head.

Denise rode the wave of her anger all the way to the bank of elevators on the far wall. She stabbed the Down button with her index finger and tried to calm the roiling in her stomach while she waited what seemed forever for the car to arrive.

Finally, a bell chimed and the doors soundlessly slid open. As she stepped into the elevator, she saw her father striding out of her office. Every secretary in the room stared at him, but he didn't even notice their curiosity.

Looking after her, he shouted, "Denise!"

But the elevator doors closed before she was forced to acknowledge him.

"It's the accountant again, isn't it?" Bob Dolan asked as he watched Mike storm around the service bay. The other two mechanics on duty had opted for an early lunch, not that Bob blamed them any. In the space of a few weeks, their easygoing boss had turned into Godzilla. The last few days had been especially rough.

Mike's angry strides slowed long enough for him to throw an icy glare at his friend. "Stay out of it, Bob."

"Love to, Ryan," the other man said and leaned one beefy forearm on a workbench. "But you keep draggin' it in to work every day. You know your mechanics are set to quit?"

Mike gritted his teeth to keep from shouting.

Bob went on. "Even Tina's about ready to run you down with one of your own bikes."

He knew he had been making everyone around him miserable. But he was just too mad to care at the moment.

"Let 'em quit," Mike snapped. "As for Tina, if she can put up with you for twenty some years, she can damn sure put up with me."

"Maybe, but you're not as good lookin' as me, either."

Mike snorted a laugh, despite his foul temper.

"What's goin' on, buddy?"

He pulled a deep breath into his lungs, exhaled on a rush and shook his head. "I really loused things up this time."

"The accountant?"

"Denise."

"Right." Bob nodded. "What about her?"

Mike looked at him. "She's pregnant."

A few seconds ticked by before Bob pushed away from the bench and grinned. "That's great, Ryan."

Mike scowled

"Isn't it?" Bob asked.

"I don't know," he admitted, disgusted with himself, Denise, the situation, everything. He had done as she asked. He had stayed away. Given her time to think. But it had been five long days and there still was no word from her.

Was he supposed to just stand on the sidelines forever while she decided what she was going to do with *his* kid?

He didn't even sleep anymore. Every night, he ended up lying in a bed where he could still feel her presence, staring at a silent phone. Nothing was being solved this way, couldn't she see that?

"She won't talk to me, Bob. Says she needs time to think. Well dammit, how *much* time?"

"Have *you* been thinking?"

He snorted again. Hard to think when you're so exhausted you can barely see straight. "Trying to."

"Come up with anything yet?"

"I asked her to marry me."

A long, low whistle was Bob's only comment.

"She said no," Mike added, surprised that he could admit that humiliating fact even to his best friend.

Bob ducked his head to hide a small smile, but Mike saw it anyway.

"There's nothin' funny about any of this."

"I guess not," the other man conceded. "But I

seem to remember a fella standing in the hot desert sand, swearing to anybody who would listen that *he* was never getting married.''

Mike smiled briefly and shook his head. "Yeah, I remember him too. But that fella didn't have a baby coming. And that fella hadn't met Denise Torrance yet, either.''

"So, did you tell her you love her?''

He shot a wild look at his friend. Love? Who the hell said anything about *love?* Love didn't have to come into any of this. It hadn't been love that had created that baby. It had been pure, old-fashioned, need. "I never said I loved her.''

"So you *don't* love her?''

Instantly, images of Denise filled his mind. They were each so clear, he could almost smell her perfume, feel her hand in his. He recalled the feel of her sitting behind him on the bike, her thighs aligned with his. He saw her again as she had been that night in his kitchen, before they went to the beach. She had looked so right there. It had all felt so natural, talking to her there in his house where usually the silence was enough to drive him out onto the highway for a fast ride on his Harley. In memory, he heard her sighs, tasted her lips and felt her arms slide around his waist as they set off on an adventure. His breathing quickened and his throat was suddenly dry and tight. Was that love?

"I didn't say I don't love her, either.''

"Hell, Ryan, what *are* you saying?''

"I'm saying…'' Mike paused and searched for the right words. Words he could live with. Words to describe the only truth he really knew so far. "I'm saying I *want* her. And I want that baby. Isn't that enough?"

Bob scratched his beard and squinted at him. "I'm not the one you should be asking."

Mike kicked at a stack of tires, smiling grimly when the black rubber tower swayed unsteadily. "Aren't you listening? I can't ask her anything. She won't talk to me."

Just like always, Bob ignored Mike's temper and asked thoughtfully, "Since when do you take no for an answer?"

"Lately, I guess." This being fair and gentlemanly was for the birds. What he should have done was pushed his way into her house and demanded that she listen to him. He reached up to yank the rubber band from his ponytail. When his hair fell free, he stabbed his fingers through the mass and rubbed his skull, in an effort to stop the pounding going on inside.

"Mike," Bob said softly, "I never thought you were a stupid man, until now."

Mike's head snapped up. His gaze locked with Bob's. "Back off," he grumbled.

"Not this time," his friend said. "Now, I know you decided a few years back that you weren't going to love anybody."

"Dammit, Bob."

"You can't make those kinds of rules for yourself, man. They don't work. Hell, they *can't* work. Life happens, Mike." Bob looked at him long and hard. "Somehow, this woman got past that wall you built around yourself and there's no getting her out now.''

He could argue with him, but what would be the point? The man was right, whether Mike wanted to admit it or not. Denise had sneaked up on him. She had slipped beneath all of his defenses until she had reached the heart of him. The heart he would have bet money hadn't existed anymore.

He shifted his gaze to stare blankly out the open end of the service bay. ''How do I make her see that?'' he whispered.

''How?'' Bob snorted and turned back to the workbench, his duty to his friend done. ''Man, you were a marine. Storm her beaches, buddy.''

Mike nodded to himself. Enough of this waiting around. She'd had it her way for five long days. Now, they were going to play by *his* rules. Blast it, he wasn't about to lose this war. Not when winning it meant the difference between a lifetime with Denise and a lifetime of loneliness.

The battle was about to begin.

Sitting on the floor in the middle of her living room, Denise reached for the closest stack of books and picked up the one on top.

''The Perfect Baby Through Visualization,'' she read out loud, then set the book down with a muffled chuckle. How had she ended up with *that* one?

Easy, she told herself. Go into a bookstore and ask for every book they have on pregnancy. One of the clerks had had to carry the bags to her car for her and it had taken her three trips to drag them all into the house.

"*What Every Expecting Mother Should Know,*" she muttered, then flipped through the rest of the first pile. "*The ABC's of Babies, Pregnancy 101.*" She shook her head and reached for the glass of milk she had set on the coffee table.

Glancing down at her flat stomach, Denise slid one palm across it protectively. "I'm even willing to drink *milk* for you, kiddo. I hope you appreciate it."

She took a long sip and smiled to herself. Somehow, after that fight with her father, some things had become clear to her. Oh, not *everything*. She still didn't know what to do about Mike and the feelings she had for him. But she had accepted one very important fact.

This baby was coming.

However it had happened, she had been blessed with the gift of a child. She couldn't get rid of it. Erase it as though it had never been.

Giving it up for adoption was just as impossible. Besides, there was no need for that these days. Like she had told Mike, these were the nineties. Single women had babies all the time. No one batted an eye at it anymore.

Too, she was creeping up on thirty years old. Though she hated the expression, there was something to be said for that old "biological clock" argument.

She had a job, she could support her baby and herself.

Maybe she had a job, her brain corrected. She still couldn't believe she had actually stood up to her father. A small, tentative smile curved her lips. For the first time in her life, she had shouted right back at Richard Torrance.

"And you know what?" she asked the baby. "Nothing happened. The Earth didn't open up and swallow me whole. The world didn't stop. He didn't disinherit me or have me thrown out of the office."

Amazing.

Of course, she told herself, she might very well turn up at work tomorrow to find out he *had* fired her. "But don't worry," she said and grimaced as she took a sip of milk, "we'll be okay anyway."

A deep, rumbling roar thundered along the street and Denise looked up, toward the front windows. She knew that sound too well not to recognize it. When the powerful engine sliced off, silence fell over the room.

"Daddy's here," she muttered and pushed herself to her feet.

Walking to the door, she reached for the brass knob and paused before turning it. Was she ready to talk to him? Was she ready to tell him that she would be keeping their child and raising it alone?

Well, why not? she asked herself. She had already faced down her father for the first time ever and survived it. How much harder could it be to talk to Mike?

"Come on, Denise," he said from the other side of the door. "I know you're there. I went by your office. Your secretary told me you went home."

He had gone to the office? She tried to imagine it—an angry biker facing down a room full of secretaries and accountants.

"Dammit, Denise," he continued, his voice deepening. "I have to see you."

Her heartbeat jumped into triple time. Deliberately, she tried to regain control of herself as she turned the knob and pulled the door open. "Hello, Mike."

He didn't wait for an invitation. He stepped into the house, closed the door behind him and faced her.

"When were you going to call me?" he asked. "It's been five days."

"I know," she said and turned her back on him to walk into the living room. As she hurried to the couch, she tried not to look at the floor. The floor where they had made love so passionately that they had created a new life. "I'm sorry, but I needed some time."

He stopped just inside the room. His gaze drifted across the carpet and she felt a flush of heat rise up inside her. He was doing it deliberately. Trying to remind her of that incredible night. It was working.

"What happened to our original agreement?" he asked quietly.

"What agreement?"

"To make decisions *together?*. As *friends?*"

She did remember that agreement. But things had changed. They weren't friends. They weren't lovers anymore, either. So, what did that leave? Parents?

"I've already made a decision," she said and took a deep breath to steady her racing pulse.

"Really?" He folded his arms over his chest, braced his feet wide apart and asked, "Do I get to know what it is?"

"I'm keeping the baby."

A heartbeat of time passed and she thought she saw a flicker of relief cross his face, but it was gone so quickly, she couldn't be sure.

"Good," he said.

"You approve?"

"Hell, yes. I approve. It's *my* kid we're talking about, here."

A shiver raced through Denise. Whatever he felt about her, he clearly cared about his child. Would he eventually fight her for it?

He glanced down at the stack of books on the floor and one black eyebrow lifted as he noted a particular title. With a few quick steps, Mike crossed the room, bent down and picked up the book in question. *"Being a Single Parent?"* he asked.

She heard the ice in his voice and fought it with some coolness of her own. "I thought I should start studying."

"On how to raise my baby alone?"

"Mike…"

"No, Denise, it's my turn to talk now." He dropped the book onto the fallen pile and walked to the sofa. Standing in front of her, continued. "I'm not going to let you walk out of my life without a backward glance."

"Don't do this, Mike. We both know that getting married isn't the answer."

"How do we know that?" he shouted, frustration

straining his voice. "You won't talk to me about it. What the hell is so awful about marrying me?"

She scooted farther down the couch, then stood up, a good three feet away from him. She couldn't seem to think straight when he was close to her and if she ever needed to be able to think, now was the time.

"Mike…" she began, and tried to sound reasonable. "We have nothing in common. You said so yourself on that very first night. You said you didn't want anything that came tied up in a neat little package."

"Quit throwing my own words back at me."

"But they're good words, Mike. They make more sense than what you're saying now."

"Things have changed, Denise."

"What? The baby?"

"Of *course* the baby."

"That's not a good enough reason to get married, Mike. In fact, it's a lousy reason to do it."

"Ordinarily," he hedged, "maybe I'd agree with that. But not now."

"Why?"

Couldn't he see how hard he was making everything? Why couldn't he just to away and let her find a way to live without him?

"Because I care for you, dammit!"

Her gaze locked with his. "Me?" She squeezed the words past a tight throat. "Or your baby?"

"Both of you." He took a long step toward her, but she moved back, staying out of his reach. "Why is that so hard to believe?"

"Because," she said softly, "before we knew about the baby, there was no talk about forever. In fact, I think you said something about 'just two grown-ups who share something incredible.'"

"Was I lying?"

She paused and gave him a sad smile. "No, you weren't. But that's not enough, either."

"Denise, I know you love me."

She inhaled sharply and felt the sting of tears in her eyes. "I never said that."

"Yeah, you did," he said quietly. "Once. In your sleep. The night before we found out about the baby."

One tear escaped from the corner of her eye and rolled along her cheek. She reached up and brushed it away. "Sleep talking doesn't count."

"Fine," he whispered. "Say it now. Or deny it."

Ten

Mike held his breath. If she *did* deny it, he didn't have a clue what his next move would be. Odd, that a man who had never wanted love, now found himself hoping to God that he would hear those three words.

"Fine," she said and her voice cracked. "I love you."

Relief crashed over him like a tidal wave.

"But it doesn't matter," she said quickly, shattering the fragile sense of hope building in his chest.

"Of course it matters." He took another step toward her, but she shook her head, warding him off. "When you come down to it, that's *all* that matters."

She laughed shortly. A small, grim chuckle that sent a chill of foreboding up Mike's spine.

"No, it's not, Mike," she said in a strangled tone.

"What are you talking about?"

"I won't make the mistake my mother did," she blurted. "I won't marry the wrong man."

"The wrong man? What's that supposed to mean?"

Pacing now, she marched back and forth across the room and Mike's gaze followed her every step. He noted the tension in her body and wanted to go to her. But first he had to know what he was fighting against.

"My parents," she muttered. "They were miserable together. Oh, my mother loved him, but that wasn't enough to make either of them happy. He should never have gotten married. My father wasn't *meant* to marry and have a family." She turned her head to look at him. "Just like you."

"Wait a minute." It was one thing to be hanged for your own sins...but he wasn't about to be strung up because her father was an ass.

"No. You said from the beginning that you didn't want love. Or a family." She took a deep, shuddering breath.

Damn, he had said way too much that was now coming back to haunt him. "I was wrong."

She shook her head. "No, you were honest. Which is more than you're being now."

That stung. He was being as truthful with her as he knew how to be. Fine, maybe he wouldn't have leapt at marriage before he had known about the baby. But situations change. People change—if they wanted to badly enough.

"You're talking about love and marriage and the only reason you're proposing is because of the baby."

Her features tight, her eyes sparkled with a sheen of tears he knew she had no intention of surrendering to.

"Fine, maybe that's true. Maybe I did propose because of the baby. But dammit, Denise, that's not saying I would never have proposed."

"Like I said," she whispered. "You're not being honest now. Not with me. Not with yourself."

Honesty wasn't always what it was cracked up to be. He had seen a lot of people destroyed by truths that should have stayed dead and buried. But blast it, if she wanted it, she would have it.

"Honest?" he snapped. "You want honest? All right, honey, here's honest." He knew he should shut up now, but he couldn't. Words he had kept locked away inside him for almost ten years came pouring out in a flood of frustration. "Back when Uncle Sam deployed me and a few hundred thousand of my closest friends to the desert, I had a chance to see love work. Up close and personal. In fact, I saw enough to convince me that loving *anybody* was a one-way ticket to pain."

"What are you talking about?"

"I'm talking about watching kids risking their lives, never knowing when they lay down to go to sleep, if they'd get up in the morning." He rubbed one hand across his jaw as memories tumbled into his mind. Memories he had worked hard at forgetting. "Those same kids lived from mail call to mail call. Grabbing at letters from their *loved ones* like they were the last life raft leaving the *Titanic*."

"Mike…"

He ignored her and started pacing himself, unable to hold still under the barrage of images rushing through his brain. "You wanted to hear this," he said angrily and wasn't sure if his anger was directed at her or himself. Either way, it was too late to stop the flood of memories and way past time that he dealt with them. "After mail call, I watched those same kids—*soldiers,* dammit—break down and cry because somebody back home decided that their *love* wasn't as strong as they had thought. Wives, husbands, sweethearts, it didn't matter." He snapped her a look and wasn't assuaged by the glitter of pain in her eyes. "Love destroyed all of them more completely than any enemy's bullet could have."

His features tight and pale, he said brokenly, "Love isn't only a gift, Denise. It can be the most powerful weapon in the world."

"Mike…"

He shook his head and spoke quickly to cut her off. "It wasn't just the Dear John or Dear Jane letters. Hell, a soldier practically *expects* those damn things." A bitter smile lifted one corner of his mouth briefly. "Amazing how quickly *love* fades when it has to cross a few thousand miles."

She took a step closer and one tear escaped to roll slowly down her cheek.

Mike kept talking. "The worst was seeing young men and women die and knowing that somewhere back home, someone they loved would die, too. Not a nice, clean death in battle. But a long, slow death from a wound too deep to heal.''

''So,'' she said softly, ''you vowed to never love anyone.''

''Yeah.'' He pulled in a long breath, surprised that now that he had actually voiced his fears out loud, they were a lot less intimidating. Looking into her blue eyes, he added, ''Then I met you.''

''Don't, Mike.''

''Denise, people can change their minds, you know.''

''Their minds, but not their souls.''

''What's that supposed to mean?''

''It means that my parents had things in common. They liked the same things. Knew the same people. Shared the same world and they couldn't make it work!'' She faced him, her fingers plucking at the material of her gray gym shorts. ''What chance would you and I have?''

Before he could speak, she rushed on, tears raining down her face. ''Look at us, Mike. *Really* look. I'm an accountant. You're a biker. I like my life neat and orderly. You don't even get *haircuts!* What chance would our *baby* have? I won't bring a child up in the kind of home where I was raised.'' She shook her head fiercely. ''I won't do it.''

Wounded by her outburst, he realized that he did love her. Desperately. It was the only explanation for the pain blossoming inside him.

Still, he tried to be calm. ''Your own arguments are working against you here, Denise.''

"Huh?"

"You said your folks had things in common and their marriage didn't work. Well, just maybe people need to bring a few differences into a marriage."

She shook her head, stubbornly unconvinced. He couldn't believe that he was going to lose her, not because of something *he* did, but because of the mess her parents had made out of their lives.

"You know, lady?" he said and started for her. "Maybe it's time you realized your parents made their mistakes. You can't go back and change them by refitting your life. Instead, maybe it's time you thought about being adult enough to risk making your own mistakes."

She glared at him through her tears, but he refused to be swayed by the bruised look in her eyes. He was fighting for both of them here and it looked as though he would be fighting alone.

"You and I could build something together, Denise. Something special for us *and* our kids. But you won't even give us a chance."

"Mike, you would hate living in my world."

He put his hands on her shoulders and felt her trembling.

"You're just not a suit and tie kind of guy," she went on, "and there are functions that we would have to attend. Can't you see that I'm trying to do us both a favor?"

"So you're willing to walk away from us over a suit?"

"It's not the suit itself," she whispered, looking up into his eyes. "It's everything. I like being a part of your world, Mike. The motorcycle, O'Doul's, everything. But I can't stay there. I have a life, too. One you would hate.''

''Let me be the judge of that, okay?''

She sighed.

''At least give us a chance, Denise.'' As an idea blossomed in his mind, he started talking even faster. ''Just because your mother fell in love with the wrong man, that doesn't mean that you have, too.''

She sniffed and let her head drop to his chest. Wrapping his arms around her, he held her tight, loving the feel of having her close against him again. Dammit, he wasn't going to lose her. Not now.

Not when he had finally realized that what had started as a wild, intense flirtation had become good old-fashioned *love*.

''Go out with me tonight,'' he said softly.

''Mike...''

''I'll take care of everything,'' he said. ''Just wear your best dress.'' He pulled his head back and looked down at her. One black eyebrow lifted as he added, ''I'm partial to that blue number you wore the first night we went to O'Doul's.''

She sniffed again, this time on a half smile. ''You are, huh?''

''Yeah,'' he said and just the thought of seeing her in that dress again was enough to get his body up and ready. ''That night, thought I might have to kill a couple of my oldest pals just for staring.''

It was a watery smile, but a smile.

''All right,'' she agreed. ''Tonight.''

''Six o'clock,'' he said and bent to plant a quick

kiss on her lips. He tasted her tears and vowed right then to never let her cry again. "Be ready."

The phone rang moments before six.

"Denise?"

She tensed at the sound of Richard Torrance's voice at the other end of the line. "Hello, Father."

"I..." He cleared his throat brusquely. "About this afternoon," he said.

Denise's fingers tightened on the receiver. Had he called to fire her personally?

"You said you hadn't been well lately and I wanted you to know that if you need to take a few days to regain your strength, I'll have someone cover for you."

Denise pulled the receiver back and stared at it blankly for a moment. Then she tucked it against her ear again. "Thank you Father, but that won't be necessary."

"Fine, fine..." After another long pause he began again. "As for the other nonsense about you leaving the firm."

"It wasn't nonsense, Father." She squared her shoulders hoping for courage.

"Certainly it was. This is the *Torrance* Accounting firm. You are a Torrance. I'll hear no more about it."

Surprised, she held her tongue, wondering what might be next.

"Now," he said, "as to the annual cocktail party for our clients..."

Denise smiled ruefully. Back to business. "Everything is arranged for next Saturday night."

"No loose ends?"

"None."

"Very well," Richard said, then paused. "I was going to suggest that you have Patrick Ryan escort you."

Denise gasped, more from surprise than the outrage that took a moment to build.

In that moment, her father continued. "His vacation ends this week, he has a good future with the firm...."

"No, Father."

"I beg your pardon?"

"No." She stiffened slightly, readying herself for battle. Amazing that her father was even concerning himself with her escort, she thought. "I'm going alone."

"I just thought..."

"I appreciate it," she interrupted. Strangely enough, she *did*. As far as she knew, it was the first time her father had ever taken an interest in her life. "But frankly I'd prefer to be alone."

True. If she couldn't have Mike, she didn't want a replacement. Not even an identical one.

"Of course it's entirely up to you," he conceded and Denise could hardly believe it. "As to the other, will you be coming in to work tomorrow?"

"Yes. But as I said earlier, I might be a bit late."

"Take all the time you need," he said and hung up without a goodbye.

Denise held the receiver limply in her hand. She

heard the hum of the dial tone as she stared at the phone. With her free hand, she reached up and rubbed her forehead. What was happening? Everything was changing so fast, she could hardly keep up.

Mike, talking about love and marriage.

Even *more* mind-boggling, her father, calling to inquire about her health? Trying to set her up on a date?

The doorbell rang and she jumped to her feet. Setting the phone down on its cradle, she snatched up her purse and walked to the front door. She had been so preoccupied with her father's peculiar behavior, she hadn't even noticed the sound of Mike's motorcycle.

A moment later, she knew why.

"A car?" she said, mentally cataloging yet another change in the universe. Denise looked up into Mike's face and saw him grin.

"Not *just* a car," he said. "*My* car."

"But you said you didn't do cars."

"I also said people can change."

"When did you...?"

"This afternoon," he interrupted and stroked the tip of one finger down the line of her jaw. "It's a BMW," he said unnecessarily. "Good family car. Safe. Practical."

Family. Safe. *Practical?* Mike?

She stepped out onto the porch and he reached behind her to close and lock her front door. Taking her elbow in a firm grip, he guided her down the front steps and along the walk to where the shiny new, candy apple red Beemer waited.

As he opened the car door for her, he said, "Safe and practical was for you. The racing red was for me."

"Mike, I don't know what to say."

"Good."

She glanced up at him and noted for the first time that he wasn't wearing a T-shirt, either. Not exactly a suit and tie, the white linen shirt with a banded collar and sharply pleated black slacks looked wonderful on him. His hair was pulled neatly into his ever present ponytail and the smile on his face sent her heartbeat into overdrive.

"Now," he told her, "slide in and buckle up."

Dinner was a blur, though she did recall the five-star restaurant on a cliff overlooking Dana Point. If it had meant her life however, she wouldn't have been able to testify to what she had eaten.

Now, she sat in a balcony box at the Orange County Performing Arts Center, watching their production of *Carousel*. The stylishly built hall was thrown into shadows, but for the brightly lit stage illuminating the performers. Beside her in the darkness, Mike lifted one hand and ran his index finger around the inside of his collar. When he caught her eye on him, he shrugged, gave her a smile, then returned his gaze to the stage.

Denise's mind was whirling with too much information. Too many changes had happened too quickly for her to take it all in. Her father's odd behavior. Her surprise pregnancy and the apparent redemption of the bad boy she loved.

She threw a sideways glance at Mike and found herself wondering if it could work between them. Just looking at him made her toes curl. But was that enough? Was it even enough that he cared for her, too?

Love alone couldn't make a relationship, could it? She rubbed her forehead again as the familiar music from the play swelled up into the darkened balconies. Her stomach in knots, Denise tightly folded her hands together in her lap and told herself to stop thinking. At least for the moment.

Mike had asked for this one night and she would give it to him. In the morning, she could face the same unanswerable questions again.

Decision made, she turned her attention back to the play. Silently, she watched the sad story of bad boy Billy Bigelow and the good girl who should never have married him.

"Why are we back here?" she asked as Mike pulled the BMW into his driveway.

He glanced at her, shrugged and smiled. "Thought you might like to take another bike ride with me."

Ever since the end of the play, she had been way too quiet for his peace of mind. He had hoped to prove to her that their worlds could meet. So what if he didn't use the Wave Cutter box at the Arts Center often? He would if it was important to her.

Hell, he could even get used to driving a car.

But he couldn't get used to the fact that she was so ready to walk away from him. A ride on his bike, where they would be forced into close contact, could be just what he needed.

He opened the car door, went around to her side and offered her his hand. She took it and stood up beside him.

"Mike," she said.

He didn't like the tone of her voice. It already carried the hint of goodbye in it.

"Come on," he said quickly and started for the garage. They walked up the dark, narrow drive and he released her hand to open one half of the double doors. Automatically, he stepped inside and yanked the chain that brought the lone, dim light bulb to life.

He dug into his pocket for the key, straddled the bike, then turned the powerful engine on. Looking at her, standing to one side of him, his heart began to thud painfully against his ribs.

How had this happened? How had love caught him so unaware? And so quickly? But more importantly, how could he convince her to take the risk that he was only now ready to take himself?

The rumble and vibration of the bike's engine trembled up his legs and back. She stepped closer to him and in the vague light of the overhead bulb, he watched her features tighten with a sadness that made him want to scream his frustration.

Instead, he reached out for her, grabbed her hand and pulled her in close. Dragging her head down to his, he planted his mouth on hers and gave her a kiss that demanded a response. She didn't fail him.

Returning his kiss with a desperate passion, her arms slid around his neck even as she pressed herself against him. Lifting her easily, Mike pulled her onto the bike in front of him. Perched half on his lap, half on the narrow seat, Denise moved in closer, holding him as tightly as she would have a life preserver thrown into choppy seas.

Beneath them, the engine grumbled loudly, sending vibrations bouncing along their spines. Mike's hands moved up and down her back in long caresses designed to drive her body into a fever pitch. His own body, hard and ready, pushed heavily against the fly of his trousers and Mike groaned from the back of his throat as she scooted around on his lap.

His hands dropped to her hips where he lifted the hem of that incredible dress. Bunching the fabric beneath his hands, his palms slid across the tops of her thigh-high stockings to the narrow band of her silk bikini panties.

The feel of her bare skin inflamed him and his already rock hard body tightened another notch.

"Denise," he whispered when he tore his mouth from hers.

Her head fell back on her neck as one of his hands moved between her legs to stroke that most sensitive piece of flesh. Through the sheer, silk fabric of her panties, he felt her heat and knew that he had to have her.

Now.

Eleven

He kissed the pulse point at the base of her throat and Denise arched into him, tilting her head to one side, welcoming his kiss.

His fingers moved again at her center and her thigh muscles tightened. The rumbling vibrations of the motorcycle's engine added their own trembling torture.

Denise pushed herself against his hand, letting him know silently that she wanted him as badly as he did her. It didn't matter that they were in his garage. Perched precariously on a motorcycle. All that mattered now was him and this moment when she felt so alive.

"I need you, Mike," she said on a sigh.

He groaned heavily and almost immediately, she felt the lace of her navy blue panties rip. Mike tore the fragile material from her body and Denise's hips rocked gently in an age-old invitation.

"Hold on, baby," he said and she felt him move to open the zipper of his slacks. Then his hands were on her hips, lifting her, guiding her to his hard, ready strength.

She gasped as he slowly lowered her body onto his. Denise braced herself with her hands on his shoulders and opened her eyes to stare into the shadowy green depths of Mike's gaze.

Squirming in his grasp, she tried to take more of his length inside her. He filled her so completely, she wasn't sure anymore that they could ever be separated. Her knees on his thighs, his hands at her hips, she moved on him, raising and lowering herself again and again, abandoning then reclaiming him as her own.

Her hips twisted, sending new spasms of delight spiraling within her. Mike's strong fingers kneaded her bottom. Her legs trembled and her hands tightened on his shoulders. He moved within her again and Denise smiled in the dim light. She watched his eyes slide shut as her hips rocked in a slow, rhythmic motion.

When the first tingling sensation started, low and deep, Denise's breath caught and held. Tension built slowly, creeping from her body into his as completion neared.

The heavy rasp of his breath sounded in her ear and she felt her own lungs straining for the cool night air whispering into the garage through the open door. An incredible tightness grabbed at her.

Denise's eyes squeezed shut as she concentrated on the sensations, willing them to come faster, harder.

As the first convulsive climax ripped through her, she ground her hips against him. Wrapping her arms tightly around his neck, she muffled a shout by burying her head in the curve of his shoulder.

Seconds later, she felt Mike shudder, heard him whisper her name as he emptied himself into her.

The hard, physical release left them both breathless, locked together, clinging only to each other.

Thirty minutes later, they were standing on her front porch. He took the key she gave him, opened her door and pushed it wide.

"Can I come in?" he asked.

"Sure," Denise said softly. She led the way inside, dropping her purse on a small table in the entryway before continuing on into the living room. She hit the switch plate on the wall as she went in and instantly small puddles of light erupted all around the room.

Denise walked to the sofa and plopped onto the cushions. Mike, she noticed, didn't sit down.

She looked up at him. "Mike, what happened a little while ago doesn't change anything."

"What do you mean?" His jaw tightened.

"I mean," she said and leaned back into the overstuffed fabric behind her, "sex isn't the issue here. We already know that we get along fine on that score." Absently, she smoothed the skirt of her dress across her knees. "But we have to think about the baby. What's best for her."

"What's best for the baby is having two parents."

"I agree with you."

"You do?" Both eyebrows lifted in surprise.

"Of course. Two loving parents are always preferable to one."

His gaze narrowed, sharpened on her. "Then what's the problem?"

"The problem is, you want us to be *married* and parents."

"You don't." It wasn't a question.

She shook her head and chewed at her bottom lip for a moment before speaking again. "I've been thinking about this all night...well, since the end of the play, anyway."

"Thinking about what?"

"What to do. How to handle this." She pushed up from the couch, kicked her heels off and started walking aimlessly around the room. "I don't want to keep you from your child."

"Oh, thanks."

She ignored the sarcasm and said what she felt she had to say. "And I don't want to stop seeing you, either."

"So, what's your plan?"

Denise turned around to look at him from across the room. "That we keep things as they are. Like you said when we first went out. We're two people who share something incredible...I'm not ready to give that up."

"Perfect," he muttered. "Do you remember *everything* I say so that you can throw it at me at some later date?"

"Mike."

"Dammit, Denise," he shouted, "I don't want to be a visitor in my child's *or* your life." Shoving both hands into his pockets, he glared at her. "I never thought I would say this to anyone—in fact, I had *planned* to never say it. But I *love* you."

She sucked in a gulp of air past the knot in her throat.

"I want us to be together. A family."

Shaking her head at him, she said, "If we're unhappy, the baby will be, too."

"Who says we'll be unhappy?" he demanded, pulling his hands from his pockets to throw them wide, helplessly.

"I told you about my parents."

"Forget about your folks and the stupid mistakes they made, will you?" His voice sounded raw with pain she knew she was causing.

"How can I forget? I grew up in a house where unhappiness was a way of life. *No* child should have to live like that. Especially not *my* child."

"Denise," he said through gritted teeth, "we make our own happiness. *Or* misery." Moving quickly, he walked toward her. He kept talking as he went, clearly trying to control a rapidly rising temper. "Maybe your father *was* a jerk. And maybe your mom let him get away with it."

"What?"

He snorted a choked laugh that held no humor. "If my dad tried to ignore my mother, she'd get in his face and shout until she had his attention. Same goes for him." As he got closer, she took a step backward, but bumped into the sliding glass doors and knew she couldn't go any farther. Mike stopped right beside her. Looking down into her eyes, he said, "Happiness doesn't just *happen.*"

"I know that," she snapped, looking for a way past him and coming up empty. "But there's no point in stacking the deck against yourself, is there?"

"How is loving each other a *bad* thing?" he asked tightly.

"It's not bad, necessarily," Denise muttered and took the direct approach. She shoved at his chest until he backed up. Stepping past him, she walked to the far wall and stopped to look at him from a safe distance. "It's just not enough."

"There are no guarantees, Denise. Not for anybody."

She reached up and pushed her hair back from her face.

In seconds, he had crossed the room. His hands warm and strong on her shoulders, he waited until she met his gaze to speak again. "Who are you scared of, Denise? Me? Or you?"

She pulled away from him and shifted her gaze from his. Unwilling to admit to fear and unable to deny it, she said, "I'm not afraid. I'm just trying to think with more than my hormones."

"That's it." He grabbed her elbow and turned her around to face him again. "This is all bull, Denise. All of it. If you remember everything I said, remember this, too. Sometimes you have to stop thinking and just *feel.*"

She laughed and winced at the raw, scraping sound of her own voice. "Feel? Didn't you watch the same play I did tonight?"

"What are you talking about *now?*"

"*Carousel.* Weren't you paying attention?"

He released her, shook his head and stared at her, waiting.

She had felt it all through the play's production. It had been almost like a sign. Fate, reminding her just what could happen if the wrong two people fell in love. She had tried to ignore it, but she couldn't. Denise was only surprised that Mike hadn't drawn the same conclusions.

"It was right there on the stage, Mike. It was as if someone were trying to tell us something." She wrapped her arms about herself and hung on tight. "Billy Bigelow was the wrong man for her. But she married him anyway. She let her feelings get in the way. And look what happened? He died and she mourned him forever!"

"I don't believe this, Denise." He looked up at the ceiling for a moment, then shifted his gaze back to hers. "It was a play! Fiction."

She shook her head firmly. "No, it was a sign. Don't you get it, Mike? We're just like the players in *Carousel.*"

"You're way overreacting."

"No, I'm not. You just don't want to see the similarities between us and the couple in the play."

"I am *not* Billy Bigelow, dammit! And this is real life! Our decisions aren't based on whatever some fool playwright jots down on a sleepless night." He grabbed her arms again and yanked her to him. His hands held her firmly but gently. She sensed the leashed power in him and heard his anger in his voice. She looked up into fierce green eyes. "We're real people, Denise. With real feelings and real brains to sort out our problems. We can love and be loved without a script."

"Mike, I know the difference between reality and fantasy, but you have to admit—"

"No! I don't have to admit anything beyond the fact that you're driving me out of my mind. You seem determined to push me away no matter what I say or do. I've listened to your theories and your fears and tried to be patient." He sucked in a gulp of air and exhaled just as quickly. "God, Denise, don't you think all of this scares the hell out of me, too? I've faced down bullets and screaming, heavily armed enemies with more confidence...but I'm standing here telling you that I love you. I love our baby and now *you* have to choose."

"How can I?"

Mike looked down into those wide blue eyes and saw the fear and confusion written there. He didn't know how to reach her. How to get past the years of hurt she had experienced as a child.

Maybe though, he wasn't supposed to. Maybe, he suddenly thought, it had to come from her. Denise had to be the one to put her past behind her and come to him on her own. If he pushed her into it, leaving her no way out, she would never *really* be with him.

It would take every ounce of his strength to walk

out of there. But he wasn't going to spend the rest of his life paying for the crimes of her father.

Lifting his hands, he cupped her face, letting his thumbs stroke her cheekbones as his gaze drifted over her features slowly, lovingly. He was taking a huge chance here and he knew it. But sometimes in war, you had to let the other guy think you were out of the battle. Make your opponent come to you.

"I'm not going to go along with your little plan, Denise."

She blinked a sheen of moisture from her eyes and his gaze locked on a solitary tear tracking down her cheek. His heart felt as though a giant fist were squeezing it.

"I won't be a visitor in my child's life and I won't be *just* the man who shares your bed."

Her bottom lip quivered and he felt her trembling. Fiercely, he steeled himself against surrendering to the urge to hold her, comfort her.

"I want it all. I want you and the baby and me, living in my grandparents' house at the beach." He paused to take a breath and smiled gently at her, despite the tears swimming in her eyes. "I want us to have the kind of life they had. I want to fall asleep every night with you in my arms and then wake up to your kiss." His fingers smoothed her hair back from her face and he felt, more than saw, her turn her head into his touch. "I love you," he said again and realized that it was getting easier to say all the time. In fact, he enjoyed saying it. Wanted to spend the rest of his life saying it to her.

"But what happens to us is up to you now. You

have to decide if you're going to keep running your life according to other people's mistakes.''

He bent down and pressed a soft, gentle kiss to her still trembling lips. Before he straightened up again, he added, ''We deserve a life together, Denise. You, me and our child. You can give us that life.''

''Mike—''

''Shh…'' His thumb stroked across her mouth, effectively silencing her. ''It all comes down to love, baby. Love and trust. I know you love me. But do you trust me?''

''I—''

''It's up to you, baby,'' he said, cutting her off because he couldn't risk hearing her decision now, before she had had her time to *think*. He sealed his last words with a kiss that left him aching for all the things she was denying him.

Before his courage could desert him, Mike turned and left the condo. He closed the door behind him and took the pansy-lined walkway in several long strides. Climbing aboard the motorcycle he had brought her home on, he jammed the key in the ignition then pulled his helmet on.

When the engine leapt into life, he twisted the accelerator on the handlebars, shattering the quiet on the street with an angry roar. Tossing a last glance at the condo, he told himself that this was all his fault. If he hadn't been trying to impress her, he never would have taken her to the Performing Arts Center and she never would have thought about *Carousel*.

"*Carousel,* for God's sake," he muttered in disgust. "First time I've used that box in years and they're playing *Carousel.*" He flicked the kickstand up into place and tried to ignore the memory of making love with Denise on that very bike only an hour or so ago. "Damn plays. Why couldn't it have been *The King and I?*"

Four days later, Denise walked down the hall of the Torrance Accounting firm, trying desperately to think of anything else but Mike. It wasn't working. He hadn't called. He hadn't come by.

And she missed him so much it hurt.

"Mr. Ryan called," her secretary said as Denise walked past her desk.

She stopped dead.

Hope rushed into her heart.

She had tried to keep busy. Working on the firm's upcoming cocktail party had given her enough details to worry about that her brain was constantly active. But in those occasional moments of peace, Mike's image instantly leapt into her mind. As it did every time she tried to sleep.

Haunted by thoughts of what could be as much as by her memories, Denise hardly knew which way to turn anymore. The only certain thing in her life was that she had a baby coming. A baby it was up to her to protect and provide for.

And soon, everyone would know it.

The dizziness had passed but she was just beginning to experience the thrills of morning sickness. In another few months, the baby would be showing.

Well before then, she had to make one of the most difficult decisions of her life.

To risk being hurt by Mike—or to live with the pain of being without him.

"Ms. Torrance?" the older woman asked. "Are you all right?"

Denise forced a smile. "Yes, Velma, I'm fine thanks. You said Mike Ryan called?"

Her secretary smiled knowingly and shook her head. "No, *Patrick* Ryan."

"Oh." The rush of exhilaration slipped away as if it had never been. She should have known better. Mike had made himself perfectly clear on their last night together. He wouldn't be calling her again.

He had thrown the ball into her court.

"What did Patrick want?" she asked, though at the moment, she didn't really care what Mike's twin was up to.

"It was very odd," the older woman said. "He's taking a three-week leave of absence. Asked me to have you inform your father."

"A leave of absence?"

"That's what he said."

After almost a four-week vacation, he needed a leave of absence?

"Did he leave a number?"

"Nope," the secretary shook her head again. "Just said he would keep in touch."

Denise scowled to herself. Maybe Patrick wasn't as different from his brother as she had thought. "Fine, but the next time he calls, get a number."

"Yes, ma'am."

Continuing on down the hall, Denise muttered disgustedly about men in general and Ryan men in particular.

The secretary's phone rang several minutes later. Velma smiled when she recognized the man on the other end.

"Hi, Velma," Mike said. "How is she today?"

"She seems fine. A little pale, maybe. Distracted. But busy."

Pale. Mike frowned thoughtfully and sat back on his couch, putting his feet up on the low coffee table in front of him. He hated not being with Denise. Knowing firsthand how she was feeling. But until he made her see what they had together, the best he could get was daily updates from a secretary with romance in her soul.

It wasn't enough, dammit. He had hoped to hear from Denise before this, but she was just stubborn enough to wait until after the baby was born to come to her senses. Maybe what she needed was one more push in the right direction.

"Velma," he said thoughtfully, "tell me more about this cocktail party you mentioned yesterday."

Twelve

"**I** can't believe Patrick Ryan would be so unprofessional as this," Richard Torrance muttered blackly. "To simply take a leave of absence with no thought as to how it will affect this firm."

Denise sat in the deep leather chair opposite her father's desk. "Obviously something he hadn't counted on came up."

"Something more important than his responsibilities here? To us? To his clients?"

She had been listening to her father rant now for more than ten minutes. Her head hurt. Her stomach was upset. And if she had Patrick Ryan in front of her, she would kick him in the shins. Some friend he was, leaving her to break the news of his absence.

Mike never would have done that.

She blinked, surprised as that thought shot

through her mind. It was true. Mike would have called Richard Torrance personally and told him straight out that he needed some personal time. And if her father had dared lecture him on his responsibilities, Mike would have quit on the spot.

He wasn't the kind of man to sit back and let life happen. He rushed out to meet it, refusing to be put off by dangers or fears.

It would have been interesting to see Mike and her father go head-to-head. Odd, but she had the feeling that once over the initial shock, Richard Torrance would probably like Mike. At the very least, he would respect him.

She smiled to herself. One thing she couldn't fault Mike on was his courage. He had even had the nerve and will to admit that he loved her—despite all of the ridiculous arguments she kept throwing at him.

Ridiculous?

She frowned, then slowly nodded to herself.

Yes. Denise sat up straighter in the chair. Absently, she noticed that her father was still talking, complaining about Patrick. But she didn't care. Something was happening here. Something monumental.

Looking past her father, she stared out the tall windows at the ocean beyond. On the horizon, a low bank of thunderheads gathered. A hard, cold wind made the sea choppy, but still there were at least a dozen sailboats sprinkled across the deep blue waves.

Others, unafraid to take a chance.

She swallowed hard. Her heartbeat skittered, then

began to beat in a quick double time. In the pit of her stomach, a curl of worry unwound, but she deliberately fought it down.

It was time, she decided suddenly, that she stood up and took her chances like the rest of the world. Time to stop hiding behind old fears and older wounds.

These last four days without Mike had finally taught her something. Strange that she hadn't even acknowledged it until now. Four days of emptiness were quickly balanced against the time spent with Mike.

The scales were easy to read. Even to a woman who had managed to keep blinders on for most of her life. Another smile crossed her face briefly. It didn't matter what her parents had done with their lives. It only mattered what she had found with Mike. What they could create together.

If she hadn't waited too long.

Denise jumped up from her chair.

"Where are you going?" her father barked.

"I have to leave early today," she said as she walked hurriedly to the door.

"Just wait one minute, young woman. You can't leave yet. We haven't finished—"

"Father," she said as she turned to face him. "I don't have time to explain. I'll tell you all about it another time, all right?"

"Tell me now, blast it."

The tone of voice was the same, sharp commanding tone she had always responded to. Until lately.

"No."

His mouth opened and closed rapidly, but he didn't say a word. Amazing. All she had ever really had to do was to speak up to him. Why had she always been so afraid of doing it? She had wanted him to love her. To care about her.

But how could he have? He didn't even know who she was. She had spent most of her life trying to be whoever Richard Torrance wanted her to be. Too afraid to be the person she was for fear it wasn't good enough.

Mike had been wrong about one thing. It wasn't about trust. It was about courage. The courage to ask for what you wanted and then to fight to keep it.

She wondered now if things might have been different—if her *life* might have been different—if her mother had demanded Richard Torrance's love and respect.

"Did you love my mother?" she asked abruptly.

"What?" A rush of color filled his cheeks as he fell back into his chair. He stared at his daughter as if he didn't recognize her.

He probably didn't.

"It's an easy question, father. Did you love mother?"

He looked at her for a long, silent minute. Denise tensed, not sure what she would hear.

"Yes," he said. "I did."

Relief washed through her. "Why didn't you ever spend time with us?"

He scowled and shifted his gaze from hers. Ducking his head, he picked up a sheaf of papers from his desk and busied his hands by straightening the pile.

But she had finally managed to ask the question. Now she had to hear the answer. "Father, why? Was it because of me?"

He dropped the papers and looked directly at her. Obviously horrified, he blurted, "Certainly not. You were a child, Denise. What was between your mother and I had nothing to do with you."

Nothing to do with her? At twenty-nine years old, she had made most of the decisions in her life based on what she had seen growing up.

She came back into the room, placed her palms on the edge of his desk and leaned towards him. "It had *everything* to do with me. Don't you think I ever wondered why you were never at home? Why mother was always so unhappy?"

His features twisted into a mask of pain and briefly, Denise regretted even opening the subject. But it was finally time to be honest. Long past time, really.

He flattened his palms on the desktop and stared down at the backs of his hands as if fascinated. After a long, thoughtful moment, he said softly, "Your mother was a...*delicate* woman. She seemed to prefer being off by herself." He shook his head slowly, lost in memories. "Whenever I was at home, she was forever fluttering around the house...unable to sit still a minute. Always nervous. Always tense." He sighed heavily. Regret coloring his voice, he added, "My presence seemed to upset her so that I finally just stayed away more and more."

"She loved you."

His gaze lifted to his daughter's. "She never said so."

A deep well of sadness opened inside her. Too late for them. Her parents had missed so much. Neither of them had been willing to talk to the other. To admit the truth of what they felt and to ask for what they needed.

So instead, they had spent their lives together, yet alone.

Denise pushed up from the desk and smiled at the man she had misunderstood for so long. There was no place here for blame. Not anymore. Besides, there had been enough unhappiness between the Torrances. "I love you, too, Father."

She thought she saw a glimmer of moisture in his eyes, but it was so quickly gone, she could have been mistaken.

"Then you'll tell me why you're leaving work in the middle of the day?" he asked, obviously hoping for a change of subject.

She grinned at him. "Nope."

"Denise…"

"I'll talk to you later, Father," she said and left the office, sailing through the open door. She didn't have a moment to lose.

She had already wasted four precious days.

"Where is he?" Denise asked out loud as she drove slowly past Mike's house. Again.

In the three days since finally clearing the air with her father, Denise had tried every way she knew to get in touch with Mike. She hadn't been able to find him.

He was never home when she called. Never returned her messages. She dropped by the motorcycle shop only to be told that she had "just missed Mike." He had to be deliberately avoiding her.

Now, here she was, the night of the firm's cocktail party and instead of being at the hotel welcoming their guests, she was cruising a beach neighborhood looking for Mike Ryan.

Her father was going to be furious.

Sighing, Denise turned her car around and headed for the downtown area. She might as well go and face the music. Once she had her father calmed down, she would leave the party and look for Mike again.

If he thought she was going to give up easily, he was mistaken. It might have taken her forever to make up her mind what it was she wanted…but now that she had, she wasn't about to give it up.

Music rushed out through the double glass doors and onto the circular drive outside the Sea Sprite Hotel. Denise stepped out of her car, took the parking slip from the valet and walked toward the entrance.

Crystal chandeliers hung from the ornate ceiling, spilling hundreds of watts of light on the elegantly dressed men and women attending the party. The hotel lobby, sprinkled with tapestry love seats and overstuffed wing chairs had become a meeting place where local businessmen gathered in tight knots exchanging cards.

Denise smiled, nodded to a few of her clients, and kept walking, heading for the stairs and the ballroom on the second floor. The skirt of her red silk dress swung around her knees as she climbed the marble steps, her mind still on the problem of locating Mike.

Why was he doing this? Had he changed his mind? Was he sorry now that he had ever asked her to marry him in the first place?

No. She wouldn't believe that. He loved her. He loved their baby.

Then why was he making himself invisible?

"Denise," Richard Torrance muttered as he hurried to meet his daughter at the head of the stairs. Taking her arm he led her to the edge of the ballroom where several couples were dancing already. "You're late."

"I know." Denise looked past him at the milling crowd. She usually enjoyed these annual parties. But tonight, her heart just wasn't in it. "I had something I had to do."

He waited a heartbeat for an apology that wasn't coming. Then he shook it off and said, "People have been asking for you. You'd better get in there and start mingling. Be sure to speak with Mrs. Rogers about her accounts, she…"

"I'm not staying, Father," Denise interrupted.

"What do you mean, you're not staying? Of *course* you're staying." He waved one hand at the revelers. "Even Patrick realized that he had a duty to be here."

"Patrick's here?" she asked, looking from her father into the mass of people just beyond the threshold.

"Didn't I just say so?"

"Where?" Denise asked, craning her neck to see over the heads of the people blocking the entrance to the room. Patrick? Patrick had wanted a leave of absence. He wouldn't have returned simply to attend a cocktail party, no matter how important.

Would he?

"He's in there somewhere." Richard paused and pointed at a small group of men. "There. In the gray suit."

Denise looked at the man's back. Short, black hair. Wide shoulders. Nicely tailored suit. It *could* be Patrick, of course. She couldn't be sure until he turned around.

"No more of this *leaving* nonsense, Denise," her father said hotly. "This is the Torrance party. *You* are a Torrance."

Denise smiled at him. "For now," she said.

"What is *that* supposed to mean?"

She kept her gaze fixed on the tall man in gray. Silently willing him to turn and look at her, she went on talking to her father. "You might as well know everything," she said. "Someone asked me to marry him a week ago."

"What?" Confusion settled on Richard's features. "Who?"

She tore her gaze from the man just inside the

ballroom and looked directly at the older man standing beside her. Courage, she thought. Taking a deep,
steadying breath, she said, "The father of my
child."

Richard Torrance's eyes widened until she
thought they might pop from his head. His brow
furrowed and bright splotches of color stained his
cheeks.

A couple of weeks ago, she would have been terrified. Now, she only hoped he wouldn't have a
heart attack or something.

"You're...you're..."

"Pregnant," she finished for him. "With your
first grandchild."

His jaw dropped.

Denise patted her father's arm gently. "It's all
right *Grandpa,* you'll get used to it."

"Grandpa?"

"The only problem here is," Denise said and
shifted her gaze back to the man in gray. He seemed
to have drifted a bit closer, though his back was still
turned to her. "I don't know if he still wants me."

"And why wouldn't he?" Richard wanted to
know.

She threw him a quick smile. "Because I drive
him crazy, he says. I kept insisting that we were all
wrong for each other. That he was the wrong man
for me."

"Well, is he?" Richard demanded.

"No, Father," she said, her gaze locked on the
man in gray. "He's the only *right* man for me."

"Well then, he'll do the right thing by you, too."

"Whether he does or not, you should know that I'm going to raise this baby. All alone, if I have to."

"Don't be foolish, Denise," her father snapped, loudly enough that several heads turned in their direction.

She looked up at her father, but before she could speak, she heard a familiar, deep voice say, "You can't talk to her like that."

Denise and her father turned at the same time to watch Patrick Ryan walk up to them, a furious scowl on his features.

"This is *family* business, Patrick," Richard said. "I'll thank you to keep out of it."

A small crowd formed around them.

Denise noticed them, but didn't care. She only had eyes for one man. Mike Ryan, masquerading as his own twin. She watched his jaw twitch with the effort to keep from shouting at her father.

Her gaze moved over him quickly. He had cut his hair, bought a suit and was pretending to be someone he wasn't all for her sake. Shame rippled through her. Because she had been a coward, the man she loved had given up a part of himself to be what he thought she wanted him to be.

"You didn't have to cut the ponytail," she whispered.

"It doesn't matter," he answered, oblivious to the people around them.

"Everything about you matters," she countered and instinctively walked toward him. Reaching up, she pulled his head down close and kissed him. Hard.

Mike fought down the urge to hold her. To grab her to him and keep her so tightly against him that she would never be able to get away again. It had been hell, avoiding her for the last three days. But he'd had to.

They had had to face each other at this cocktail party. With her in her element. He had thought it would be the one sure way to know if she wanted him. But it had been a stupid idea. Nothing was solved. Yes, she was kissing him in front of everyone. But was it only because tonight, he looked the part of the rising young businessman?

Denise finally pulled back from him and looked up into his eyes. He stared down into those blue depths and felt his soul move into hers.

Smiling, she reached for his tie and quickly undid the careful Windsor knot. Then she unbuttoned his collar button and lifted one hand high enough to ruffle her fingers through his perfect haircut.

"I love you," she whispered, speaking directly to his heart. "The *real* you. Motorcycles, black leather, ponytail and all."

A tentative smile lifted one corner of his mouth. "You don't need suits and ties in your life?"

She shook her head "I never want you to change for me, Mike. All I want is for you to love me."

His chest tightened. Pride and love swelled up inside him as he reached up to yank the hated tie from his neck. Tossing it into the air, he grinned. "No problem, baby," he said, through a suddenly dry throat.

"Denise, are you going to tell me what is going

on here?'' Richard sounded exasperated, but surprisingly calm, all things considered.

"Dad," she announced loudly, taking one of Mike's hands and setting it at her waist, "I'd like you to meet *Mike* Ryan. He owns Ryan's Custom Cycles and is probably the best bike mechanic in the state." She grinned at her father then. "He's also Patrick's brother and the man I'm going to marry—if he'll still have me."

For an answer, Mike spun her around in his arms. Looking deeply into her eyes, he spoke quietly, not caring who heard. "I didn't want to love you, Denise. But now I don't want to live without you." He smoothed his fingertips down the line of her cheek. "Marry me, baby. Marry me and let me love you forever."

Tears swam in her eyes. He held his breath, waiting. When she nodded, he yanked her into his arms and bent his head to claim a kiss designed to sear her soul.

A woman in their audience sighed plaintively.

At last, Mike lifted his head to smile down at his almost wife.

"Custom Cycles, eh?" Richard said, loudly enough to get his soon-to-be son-in-law's attention. "You could probably use a good accounting firm, my boy."

Mike grinned. At least the man had the sense to surrender when there was nothing left to do. Tucking Denise close to his left side, Mike stretched his right hand out to his future father-in-law. As the other man took it in a firm shake, Mike told him, "Thanks. But I've already got a good accountant."

Silly to have waited so long to get married, Denise told herself as she turned to look up into her groom's eyes. But she'd wanted to clear all of her client's business affairs so that she and Mike could take a real honeymoon. Now she and the gorgeous, ponytailed man in the black tuxedo were just four hours away from their flight to Tahiti.

His gaze moved over her hungrily, lovingly and she felt the shock of amazement right down to her toes. Not only did he enjoy the changes her body was going through, this miraculous man actually seemed to find her swollen belly erotic. At that salacious thought, she tightened her grip on the bouquet she still held in her right hand and stretched out her left to Mike, eager to finish the ceremony and start the marriage.

He inhaled sharply as her fingers touched his. His thumb smoothed across her knuckles as the justice of the peace solemnly intoned the words that would bind Mike Ryan to this woman for the rest of his life.

She looked beautiful. Her off-white dress—she'd insisted on ivory—was cinched beneath her breasts and draped lovingly across the mound of his child. A simple wreath of yellow carnations and white daisies encircled her head, making her look like an ancient goddess of summer.

How in the hell had he *ever* gotten this lucky? he wondered and grinned down into blue eyes that held all the answers to every question he'd ever asked. Behind them, a small group of family and friends held their collective breath expectantly as Mike slid a plain gold band onto Denise's finger.

When the deed was done and all was official, they smiled at each other just before Mike gently placed his right hand on their baby. "I swear I will love you both forever," he whispered.

She covered his hand with hers and rose up on her toes. When his mouth claimed hers, Denise realized that marriage was a *very* sexy thing!

Epilogue

"Take it easy, Mr. Torrance." Tina Dolan looked up at the older man pacing around the dimly lit hospital waiting room. "She's only been in there an hour or so. We could be here all night."

"All night?" Richard paled and slumped down onto one of the hard plastic chairs littering the room. "This waiting business was a lot easier when I was a younger man," he mumbled.

The late night quiet was overwhelming. Besides the Dolans and Richard Torrance, there was only a handful of people sprinkled around the big room.

"Talk to him," Tina told her husband. "Take his mind off of things. This has got to be hardest on him, waiting for word about his only daughter."

Bob Dolan never had to be asked more than once to start talking. Getting up, he walked across the room and took the chair next to the other man. "Y'know," he said, "I've been thinking about setting up some retirement accounts for me and Tina."

Richard glanced at him from the corner of his eye.

"Not gettin' any younger, y'know. Got to get a hedge on those 'golden years'."

"That's a very good idea," Richard said and tossed an anxious glance at the double doors leading to the maternity ward.

"So, what do you think we ought to invest in? Have any good ideas?" Bob prompted the man, hoping to strike a financial nerve. From what Mike said about his father-in-law, the man *loved* to talk business. "I was thinking about maybe sinking some cash into land."

Richard's heavy gray eyebrows lifted slightly. "Property is certainly one way to go about safeguarding your future," he said. "But let me give you a few more tips...."

"C'mon baby," Mike whispered close to her ear. "You're almost there. One more good push and you'll be finished."

She looked at him and nodded. A sickly green cotton gown covered his T-shirt and jeans and he wore a matching cotton cap to cover the ponytail that was now fully grown back. She held his hand tightly and thanked God that he had wanted to be a part of the delivery. She didn't know how she would have gone through all of this without him.

Denise's breath came in short, harsh, rasping breaths. A tearing discomfort settled low in her body and every instinct she possessed told her to push. But she was so tired.

Not only was the baby arriving two weeks early, but the time from the first indication of a labor pain to this overwhelming pressure had taken only three hours. She had always thought a first baby took forever to be born. She had thought she would be prepared.

She wasn't.

"Mike," she gasped in the brief interval between pains, "what if we screw up? What if we're lousy parents?"

He grinned at her. "Are you kidding?" he asked. "We're going to be *great!*"

"All right, Mrs. Ryan," the doctor said. "Get ready to bear down and see your baby."

"It's two weeks early," Denise managed to say as another pain began to build deep within her. "Will it be all right?"

Kathryn Taylor smiled gently. "Two weeks is nothing to worry about."

"Oh, Mike," Denise complained, "your parents will be so disappointed that they weren't here. And your brothers, too."

"Patrick's here," he soothed her. "As for the others, when they do arrive, they'll have the pleasure of meeting the baby without having to wait."

The pain grew and blossomed, opening inside her, making her strain and grit her teeth for battle.

"I see the baby's head, Denise," the doctor crowed. "Almost there."

Denise's breath came in short, hard gasps. Concentrating on her task, she only nodded to the doctor.

"Now," Mike asked as he braced her into an almost sitting position, "aren't you glad we waited to find out the baby's sex?"

Denise didn't answer him. She was far too busy. She felt Mike's strong arms holding her. She heard the doctor's encouraging voice. She felt a last incredible burst of energy rush through her body and when it came, she gathered it to her, gave one last mighty effort and pushed her child into the world.

An indignant scream filled the room and someone laughed.

She looked up into Mike's green eyes and found them teary. "Did you see him?" he whispered. "It's a boy, baby. We have a son."

A son.

She turned her face into his chest and his arms came around her in a gentle, fierce hug. In moments, a nurse was there beside the gurney, holding an incredibly tiny person wrapped up in a pale blue blanket.

"Mr. and Mrs. Ryan," she said and placed the baby carefully into Denise's outstretched arms. "Meet your bouncing baby boy."

Mike leaned down, kissed his son's forehead, then turned to kiss his wife. A wife. A son.

"Have I thanked you lately?" he asked, oblivious to the rest of the people in the room.

"For what?" she said through the tears blurring her vision.

"For loving me."

"You're welcome."

"Hey, Mike!" A deep voice called from the doorway.

They turned to see Patrick's head poked around the edge of the delivery room's double doors.

"Pat!" Mike shouted.

"Get out of here right now," one of the nurses ordered.

Patrick only laughed at her. "So, what is it? Boy? Girl? *Triplets?*"

Denise groaned dramatically.

Mike said proudly, "It's a boy."

The nurse rushed forward flapping a surgical towel at Patrick as if she were a bullfighter in the ring.

Immediately, Patrick pulled his head back. But not before shouting, "I'll go tell everybody. I'll let *you* call Mom and Dad!"

Turning back to his family, Mike shook his head and said ruefully, "How could we ever screw this up and when we have so much help?"

Denise accepted the kiss he gave her, then handed him his son. Mike held the tiny bundle as if his son were made of spun glass. When he looked at her through eyes that were filled with teary pride and happiness, Denise knew that sometimes loving the *wrong* man is the only *right* thing to do.

* * * * *

*Maureen Child continues to sizzle with
Desire! Look for her upcoming*
BACHELOR BATTALION *series
beginning in September of 1998!*

DIANA PALMER
ANN MAJOR
SUSAN MALLERY

RETURN TO WHITEHORN

In **April 1998** get ready to catch the bouquet. Join in the excitement as these bestselling authors lead us down the aisle with three heartwarming tales of love and matrimony in Big Sky country.

A very engaged lady is having second thoughts about her intended; a pregnant librarian is wooed by the town bad boy; a cowgirl meets up with her first love. Which Maverick will be the next one to get hitched?

Available in **April 1998**.

Silhouette's beloved **MONTANA MAVERICKS** returns in Special Edition and Harlequin Historicals starting in February 1998, with brand-new stories from your favorite authors.

Round up these great new stories at your favorite retail outlet.

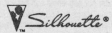

Take 4 bestselling love stories FREE

Plus get a FREE surprise gift!

Special Limited-time Offer

Mail to Silhouette Reader Service™

P.O. Box 609
Fort Erie, Ontario
L2A 5X3

YES! Please send me 4 free Silhouette Desire® novels and my free surprise gift. Then send me 6 brand-new novels every month, which I will receive months before they appear in bookstores. Bill me at the low price of $3.49 each plus 25¢ delivery and GST*. That's the complete price and a savings of over 10% off the cover prices—quite a bargain! I understand that accepting the books and gift places me under no obligation ever to buy any books. I can always return a shipment and cancel at any time. Even if I never buy another book from Silhouette, the 4 free books and the surprise gift are mine to keep forever.

326 SEN CF2S

Name _____ (PLEASE PRINT)

Address _____ Apt. No. _____

City _____ Province _____ Postal Code _____

This offer is limited to one order per household and not valid to present Silhouette Desire® subscribers. *Terms and prices are subject to change without notice. Canadian residents will be charged applicable provincial taxes and GST.

CDES-696   ©1990 Harlequin Enterprises Limited

BEVERLY BARTON

Continues the twelve-book series— 36 Hours—in April 1998 with Book Ten

NINE MONTHS

Paige Summers couldn't have been more shocked when she learned that the man with whom she had spent one passionate, stormy night was none other than her arrogant new boss! And just because he was the father of her unborn baby didn't give him the right to claim her as his wife. Especially when he wasn't offering the one thing she wanted: his heart.

For Jared and Paige and *all* the residents of Grand Springs, Colorado, the storm-induced blackout was just the beginning of 36 Hours that changed *everything!* You won't want to miss a single book.

Available at your favorite retail outlet.

Silhouette Books

is proud to announce the arrival of

A MOTHER'S GIFT

This May, for three women, the perfect Mother's Day gift is mother*hood!* With the help of a lonely child in need of a home and the love of a very special man, these three heroines are about to receive this most precious gift as they surrender their single lives for a future as a family.

Waiting for Mom
by Kathleen Eagle
Nobody's Child
by Emilie Richards
Mother's Day Baby
by Joan Elliott Pickart

Three brand-new, heartwarming stories by three of your favorite authors in one collection—it's the best Mother's Day gift the rest of us could hope for.

Available May 1998 at your favorite retail outlet.